Sky Guys
to
White Cat

by Beatrice Gormley

illustrated by
Emily Arnold McCully

DUTTON CHILDREN'S BOOKS   NEW YORK

Library of Congress Cataloging-in-Publication Data

Gormley, Beatrice.
    Sky guys to white cat / by Beatrice Gormley; illustrated by Emily
Arnold McCully.
        p. cm.
    Summary: Fifth-grader Alison tries to balance problems with her
best friend and the incredible fact that aliens are communicating
with her cat.
    ISBN 0–525–44743–1
    [1. Science fiction. 2. Friendship—Fiction. 3. Cats—Fiction.]
I. McCully, Emily Arnold, ill. II. Title.
PZ7.G6696Sk 1991   91-364
[Fic]—dc20   CIP
                                                           AC

Published in the United States by Dutton Children's Books,
a division of Penguin Books USA Inc.
375 Hudson Street, New York, New York 10014

Designer: Carol McDougall

Printed in U.S.A.   First Edition
10 9 8 7 6 5 4 3 2 1

to my cat Claude,
without whose help this story
could not have been written

B.G.

Contents

The Beginning

The Aliens Arrive

Settling the spacecraft into an orbit above the blue green planet, Commander Xorple reached out a tentacle to turn on the light repellers. Now the explorers from the system of the giant red star Aldebaran were protected. If there were any intelligent beings on the planet below, the light repellers would prevent them from seeing the spaceship.

Instruments Operator Phtui leaned forward in his canlike rester—not a chair, because the hill-shaped, butterscotch-colored Aldebarans had no rear ends—to peer through the remote scanner.

A likely life-form directly below, Commander, he signed to Xorple with his side tentacles.

In the field of the scanner, a small gray four-legged creature made its way across a flat stretch of green.

Xorple's rubbery yellow brown eyelids sank reprovingly. *Only the psychic sensor can tell whether this life-form will serve our purposes,* she signed back.

1

Phtui's snail-like foot clenched with indignation, but he signed nothing. Although this was Phtui's first mission, he considered himself well trained in the procedure for exploring new planets. The first step was to find the dominant life-form and harness it to do the exploring for the Aldebarans. Phtui knew, without being reminded, that the dominant life-form was supposed to give out a high level of psychic energy.

Activating the remote psychic sensor, Phtui poked his two minor tentacles, used for sensing rather than grasping, into the jacks. Immediately he sensed from the creature below the long, confident pulses of a dominant life-form.

This is it, Commander, he signed.

You are sure?

No doubt about it. This creature sends out the vibrations of one who knows it is superior.

Commander Xorple blinked a nod, then swiveled in her rester to program the small, automated capture craft. The capture craft, also shielded by light repellers, would pick up the gray creature and bring it to the main ship, where the Aldebarans would Collar it. Other individuals of this species would be found, and they, too, would be Collared. Then the stage of exploration by remote control could begin.

·1·

Guess What!

The afternoon was cool and drizzly, but the weather wasn't keeping Alison Harrity from enjoying the Rushfield Fourth of July parade. Sitting on a fence with her friend Denise Farino, watching the bands and the acrobats and the floats roll by, she'd been thinking about her good news. The secret felt sweet and juicy in the back of her mind, like the wisps of cotton candy melting in her mouth.

As the last float rolled by, Alison offered her cotton candy to Denise. "Guess what!"

Pulling off a pink strand, Denise raised her eyebrows. "What? A new *Weekly Informer* is out?" The *Weekly Informer* was a tabloid paper that Denise and Alison liked to read together.

"No . . ." Alison laughed. It was even more exciting, now that she was actually telling Denise. "I mean, maybe there is a new *Weekly Informer* at the 7-Eleven, but this is much better." She paused to let

3

the suspense build up. "I'm getting my orange-striped kitten today!"

"Your kitten?" Denise's voice squeaked, and she pitched so far forward that she had to grab the fence railing to keep from falling off. "Today? Can I come?"

"Sure." A giggle bubbled out of Alison's throat. "I said you could, when I got my kitten."

"Yes!" Denise leaned over to give Alison a high five. They both lost their balance and slid down from the fence, laughing.

Then Alison caught sight of Marvin Smith, an eighth-grade boy, farther down Main Street. It was easy to pick out Marvin in a crowd, because he looked so much like Curious George. "Whoops, there goes Marvin, leaving the parade. We have to follow Marvin and Maureen to the Thompsons' house, because that's where this kitten—"

Alison saw that Denise wasn't listening. She was looking across the street, but in the direction of the vanishing parade.

"Hey, there's Sonia." Denise waved with her hand high in the air. "Didn't she look mature on that football float, in her cheerleader outfit? Did you notice Sonia looks a lot like Heather Hartley—you know, the girl who gets scalped in *High School Horror?*"

Alison couldn't imagine why Denise was interested in Sonia Best. Alison knew who Sonia was, of course. She was that girl in the other fifth-grade class who'd worn huge dangly chartreuse earrings, like plastic saucers, to school last year. She'd also passed around a picture of some nearly naked rock star. Alison hadn't

4

seen the picture, but all the kids had been talking about it. "In very poor taste," the teacher had said as she took the picture away.

"What did you wave to Sonia for?" Alison asked Denise. "Now she's coming over here. We have to go."

Sonia was pushing her way through the people milling around the street. As she turned this way and that, she swung her pom-poms and twitched her short, twirly skirt. Had Sonia really gotten curvy hips, wondered Alison, or was that just the way the cheerleader skirt made her look? Her legs were as skinny as ever, but glossy—she must be wearing panty hose.

"Yo, Denise!" called Sonia, raising a pom-pom.

Alison grinned, thinking how much the rippled, messy pom-poms looked like Sonia's hair. She seemed to be shaking a wig in each hand.

Denise's round face beamed as Sonia came up to them. "I can't wait for jazz dancing to start tomorrow, can you?" breathed Denise.

"Yeah—it's going to be so mature. The teacher dances in the dinner-theater shows, it said in the booklet." Sonia did a few steps to one side, then to the other.

"That's the ball-and-chain step," Denise explained to Alison. "Sonia's picked up some jazz dancing steps, just from watching TV. Our class is going to put on a show, with costumes and everything, at the end. It might be on Rushfield TV. It's too bad you signed up for chess instead of jazz dancing, Alison."

Before Alison could answer, Sonia said casually, "I don't know." She swung her pom-poms and glanced from Alison's faded jeans to her own twirly skirt. "The teacher says you have to have a kind of *flair* for jazz dancing."

"Well, you have to have another kind of *flair* for chess," said Alison. "I won the fifth-grade chess tournament, remember? That's why the teacher let me into intermediate chess."

"Oh, really?" Sonia's made-up eyes opened wide. "I thought for getting into chess you just had to be a geeky boy." Then she slapped her hand over her mouth as if she hadn't meant to say that and pushed her masses of moussed and scrunched-up hair over her sharp features as if she were dying of embarrassment. "Guess not! Sorry."

Denise burst into a loud giggle, then clapped her hand over her own mouth with an uneasy look at Alison.

Alison couldn't believe what was happening: Denise acting so friendly toward Sonia, a girl Alison would never want to talk to in the first place. And Alison couldn't believe she, Alison, was standing there taking it. "I have to go get my kitten," she said curtly. "Bye."

Without waiting to see if Denise was coming, Alison stalked off down the street. Now Marvin was out of sight in the throngs of parade-goers. She'd have to hurry to make sure to get to the Thompsons' while he was still there.

Before she'd passed even a block of the big white houses on Main Street, though, Alison heard panting behind her and then Denise's voice. "A kitten would be a good mascot for the club, don't you think?"

Alison turned to give Denise an indignant look. "When did you get to be such great friends with Sonia Best?"

"You shouldn't get so mad," said Denise, still panting to catch up. "She didn't mean *you* were a geek. Anyway, I just talked to her while we were signing up for jazz dancing last week, that's all. She's going to be one of the most popular girls in the sixth grade, you know."

"Popular! Not if she acts like that."

"Not 'popular' like everybody thinks you're nice," said Denise patiently. " 'Popular' like everybody knows you're mature."

Alison gave Denise a puzzled glance. There was that word, *mature*, again. Denise and Sonia were using it in an odd way, as if it meant "wonderful."

But Denise seemed to want to get off the subject of Sonia. "So why are we following Marvin Smith to get your kitten? I thought you were going to get it at the cat shelter."

"No, this is better." As they weaved their way through the crowd under the line of old maple trees, Alison explained. Marvin had come by the Harritys' yesterday to see if Maureen, Alison's older sister, would help him with his cat-sitting business. One of his customers was the Thompsons, who lived just over the hill from Alison and her family.

"I tried to tell him I'd be a better cat-sitter than Maureen, because she didn't even take care of the gerbil she used to have," said Alison. "But she wanted the money, and he said I wasn't old enough."

"Probably he likes Maureen." Denise smiled.

Alison looked at her friend in surprise. She'd thought it was just a case of eighth graders sticking together against a fifth grader, but maybe Denise was right. "Anyway, then Marvin found out I wanted a striped kitten, and he said there was a stray hanging around the Thompsons', and Mrs. Thompson wanted to find a home for it. So . . ." She grinned at Denise. "Kitten, here I come!"

The girls had reached a corner where five streets came together in a cluster of stores. Denise stopped in front of the 7-Eleven, took off her glasses, wiped the drizzle from them with a tissue, and put them back on. "Hey, there *is* a new *Weekly Informer!* I wish I'd brought more money."

"Never mind, we can come back tomorrow. We have to keep going now." But Alison couldn't resist leaning against the window to read a headline on one of the stacks of papers inside. ALIEN PLANT MUNCHES MAILMAN. Oh, boy, this was going to be good.

As they hurried on across the street and up Chestnut Hill Road, Denise said, "I've got dibs on FORMER MISS AMERICA'S SEARING SECRET."

Alison glanced at Denise, smiling. "Fine." She and Denise always picked different articles at their secret-reading club meetings. Last time Denise had wanted AMAZED MOM HAS GORILLA TWINS, and Alison had chosen PHOTOS PROVE WWII FIGHTER PLANE ON MOON. It was probably just as well that she and Denise liked different kinds of stories, so they didn't argue over who got to read them first.

"So, what are you going to call your kitten?" asked Denise. "How about Marmalade? That's a good name for an orange-striped kitten."

"No, I've already got the names picked out," said Alison firmly. "Tiger Lily if it's a girl, and Rusty if it's a boy." But she frowned a little, wondering if this kitten was going to match the picture on Denise's notepaper, a cute little orange tiger kitten sniffing a flower. Marvin hadn't actually said the kitten was orange. He'd just said it was striped.

Well, it must be orange. This kitten waiting for Alison at the Thompsons' *had* to be the perfect kitten for her. Why else would it turn up like that, just when she was supposed to get her kitten?

Hiking up the steep curves of Chestnut Hill Road, the girls fell silent to save their breath. They passed Alison's house, then trudged over the hill under the dripping chestnut trees. Finally, there was the Thompsons' mailbox.

"There's Marvin and Maureen, just going in now." Alison nodded toward the front door. Marvin had to show Maureen where the cat food and other stuff was so she could start cat-sitting tomorrow, Alison supposed.

"Where are you going?" asked Denise as Alison started across the wet lawn. "Isn't the kitten in the house?"

"No." Alison stepped through the row of peonies separating the front yard from the back. "Marvin said Mrs. Thompson couldn't let it inside, because her cat hates other cats."

"So it has to live outside?" asked Denise indignantly. "Poor little Tiger Lily!"

The girls stopped beside an upside-down wading pool and gazed around the backyard. The lawn, bordered by a half circle of horse-chestnut trees, was empty.

"I don't see any kitten," said Denise, wiping the mist off her glasses again. "Unless it's hiding under the pool."

They stooped to peer under the wading pool, propped up on one side by a sand bucket. Nothing except a rubber ducky and a couple of toy boats.

But what was that meow coming from the edge of the yard? Alison stood up and squinted toward the trees. "Look, a white cat in the weeds."

Denise squinted, too, at the tall weeds on the other side of the trees. "There's something white. But that couldn't be Tiger Lily."

Alison heard the sliding door at the back of the house and turned to see Marvin leaning out. His forehead was drawn together in a frown. Marvin certainly looked like a monkey, thought Alison, although he was the smartest kid in the intermediate school.

"Hey, where's the kitten you—" began Alison.

But Marvin, not listening, pointed past Alison. "There she is, the Thompsons' cat! Grab her!"

Alison whirled to see the white cat streaking across the lawn toward the wading pool on long, flashing legs. After it charged a snarling black moplike creature with a pushed-in face. Then the small white cat ducked under the wading pool and vanished.

"Come here, Black Beauty!" Marvin scooped up the black Persian cat just as it tried to follow the white cat under the wading pool. "Gotcha. Whew! The Thompsons' housecleaner must have let her out," he added.

The white cat cautiously poked its head out as far as the collar around its scrawny neck, peering up at Alison and the rest with wide yellow eyes. It was only half as big as the black cat, thought Alison, but it seemed determined not to be scared away.

Maureen had followed Marvin out of the house. "Nice kitty," she said to the Persian, patting it gingerly. Then, as Black Beauty hissed down at the pink nose poking out from under the wading pool, Maureen jumped back.

The white cat jerked its head back into the cave of the upside-down pool.

Marvin gave Black Beauty a little shake. "Behave, you." Black Beauty only stared and twitched her feathery tail.

"So, you going to take the kitten?" he said to Alison.

"Kitten? What kitten?"

"The one under the pool," answered Marvin. He sounded impatient. "Sharkey. What kitten did you think I meant?"

·2·

Sharkey

"Kitten!" Alison could hardly speak. "That's not a kitten. It's a regular cat."

"Yeah," Denise chimed in, "and it's not orange-striped, either, like you told Alison."

"Its tail is striped," said Maureen reasonably. She pointed to the gray-and-black-striped tail tip now poking out from under the wading pool.

"And he couldn't be more than a few months old," said Marvin. "So all right, maybe Sharkey's more like a teenaged cat than a kitten." He grinned. "Well, maybe a sixth-grade cat."

Alison didn't think Marvin's remark was funny. "I can't believe you told me there was a kitten here." Something else struck her, and she felt a fresh wave of anger. "He isn't even a stray, either. Wasn't that a collar I saw on him? And you called him Sharkey."

"Yeah," said Denise. "Strays don't have names."

Marvin frowned at Alison, as if a fifth grader had no right to question an eighth grader. "Look, argue with

Mrs. Thompson, not me. She's the one who said he was a stray. She said she called the vet and the cat shelter and put up a notice on the A&P bulletin board and asked all the neighbors, and nobody knows anything about this cat—kitten, I mean. And she's been feeding him for a week, so she's probably the one who put the flea collar on him."

Tucking Black Beauty under his arm, Marvin turned toward the house, then back again. "Her little kid named him Sharkey, don't ask me why. And I never said he was orange."

"And nobody's *making* you take him," added Maureen over her shoulder, following Marvin, "so don't have a fit."

"We should go," Denise told Alison. "This isn't the mascot we wanted for the club. It isn't even a girl cat."

Alison didn't want to go. She wanted to make Marvin apologize for giving her the completely wrong idea. And she wanted to let her sister know what she thought of her remarks about something that was none of her business. But the two eighth graders were already disappearing into the house, the sliding door shutting behind them.

Denise sighed loudly. "What a waste of time for me to walk all the way over here. And it's starting to sprinkle again." She pointed to new drops on her glasses.

"So? We're wearing slickers," said Alison absently. Something had caught her eye: a pink nose poking out from under the wading pool again. A pink nose, white whiskers, and now yellow eyes gazing up at her. "Hi, Sharkey," she said.

14

Sharkey stayed in the pool-cave, but his pink mouth opened. *Rowr?*

Alison felt a pang. Such a desperate, pleading question the cat seemed to be asking her. *Choose me?* And she'd come here to choose her cat. Only this wasn't the cat she'd planned on.

Still, Alison didn't want him to think she was mean. Stooping beside the bucket that propped up the wading pool, she held out her hand. "It's okay, Sharkey. Poor little kitty."

The cat rubbed his whiskers hard against her fingertips, and Alison felt another pang. She'd come here to get her kitten without a thought about how the kitten might feel, as if it were no more than a stuffed animal. That was what the cute orange kitten of her dreams seemed like now, a stuffed windup toy. But Sharkey, looking into her eyes and speaking to her, was as real as Denise.

"Hey." Denise stooped, too, to frown at Alison. "What are you doing? We can't use this cat for a mascot. You should pick out an orange kitten at the Humane Society shelter, like you were going to."

Alison hardly heard Denise, she was watching Sharkey so intently. His yellow eyes were fixed on her. He crept forward an inch or two, so that his gray ears and the top of his gray-striped head showed. Alison rubbed behind his ears. I shouldn't get his hopes up, she thought. He'll get the impression I'm going to take him home.

Denise sighed again. "All right, so he likes you. Now can we go?"

"Poor Sharkey," said Alison, scratching under his

15

chin. The cat's eyes shut with pleasure, and he crept forward another inch or so.

"*Sharkey!*" exclaimed Denise. "What kind of a name is that? And look at those long, skinny legs," she went on as he slunk out from under the wading pool and started arching his back against Alison's hands. "And he's a dirty white. And that striped tail, sort of tacked on."

Sharkey did look odd—as if someone had set out to make a gray tiger cat, beginning with the top of the head, but then had switched and started the stripes at the other end, the tail. In the middle, the cat-maker had run out of stripes and just left the rest of him blank.

The young cat walked around and around Alison, purring and rubbing against her. "It's not his fault he's dirty," she told Denise. "He has to live outside." She knelt on the grass, ignoring the damp seeping through her jeans, and put her arms around the cat. "And he's thin because he doesn't get enough to eat. Oh!"

Sharkey had put both front paws on Alison's knees. He hesitated, gazing into her face, then crept onto her lap.

"Look!" Alison exclaimed softly. In all the months she'd looked forward to choosing a kitten, she'd never thought that one might choose her. Now Alison felt as if she was just the kind of person Sharkey had hoped would turn up all that time he had been sneaking around in the weeds at the Thompsons', hungry and dirty and lonely.

"Alison," said Denise sharply. "You're making him

think you're going to take him home. And that would be a big mistake."

But Alison hardly heard. She looked down at the cat on her lap, and he gazed back at her with half-closed eyes. A wave of tenderness washed through her. This is what it means, she thought, when they say "Her heart melted."

Alison ran her hands over the cat's bony shoulders and back. She felt comfortable and safe, as if she, instead of the cat, were the one being petted.

"Why did you tell me to come along and help if you aren't going to listen to anything I say?" Denise burst out. "There're other things I could do with my time, you know."

Alison looked up at her friend in surprise. Denise's face was red. "Why are you getting so mad?" asked Alison.

"Because you made me leave the parade in a big rush. Because we had the perfect kind of kitten all planned. And now you're acting like you're under a spell or something. Can't you see that's not a kitten?"

Alison bent her head over the cat on her lap, and he reached one long white paw up to her chin. He was purring so hard that his ribs quivered. "What's the big difference how old he is?" she said.

Denise jumped up, her hands on her hips. "You really should give the Candy Club a chance to vote on this."

"The Candy Club?" Alison almost laughed. "The club is just you and me meeting for secret readings, except once in a while we do something with Karen.

18

No one else is in it anymore. And besides, it's my cat to pick out."

"This is the last straw." Denise jerked the hood of her slicker up over her head. "If you aren't going to listen to anything I say, I'm going home."

"Oh, don't be such a . . ." Alison let her voice trail off. Denise, standing with her hands jammed into her slicker pockets, looked hurt. After all, Denise had a point—she'd come over to help Alison pick out a kitten. She'd hurried all the way from the parade for nothing, in her view. And Alison didn't want to fight.

"Listen, don't get mad," called Alison as Denise stalked off. "Let's meet tomorrow at the 7-Eleven, okay?"

Denise stopped and turned around. She had that funny expression on her face that meant she was sure she was in the right, but she didn't really want to fight, either. "Okay," she said with a grudging smile. "Tomorrow morning? No, wait—jazz dancing starts tomorrow at eleven. Let's meet tomorrow afternoon, and then take the paper to your house for the meeting."

"Okay, but right after lunch—one o'clock," said Alison. "I have intermediate chess at three."

Denise nodded. "I'll see you at one."

19

·3·

Love at First Bite

As Denise disappeared around the corner of the house, Alison gazed down at the white cat. Her stomach seemed to float, as if she'd jumped off the high board at the town pool. For better or worse, she'd chosen her cat: a dirty half-grown white stray. Sharkey.

Rrr? Sharkey stretched a paw up to get her attention. His eyes shut as she stroked him, and she could feel the motor of his purr through her slicker.

"Let's go home," she said. Picking up the cat and holding him against her shoulder, she got carefully to her feet.

At first Alison walked gingerly, afraid the cat might try to jump out of her arms. She wished she'd brought a carton to carry him in. But Sharkey lay limply in the crook of her arm, nuzzling into her shoulder now and then. Drops of mist sprinkled the gray-striped fur that covered his head like a cap.

Carrying the cat along the curving road, under quietly dripping trees, Alison held him a little tighter. She felt that she was turning a corner in her life, a corner she hadn't expected. She'd been thinking of this summer as a straight, easy road two months long, with the big corner waiting in September: the beginning of intermediate school. She'd thought it would be a lot of fun to have her own cat, but she hadn't expected it to seem so important.

"We're almost home, Sharkey," she told him as they came over the top of the hill. "There's our house."

In the family room Alison's father was lying on the sofa while Alison's mother gave him a back rub. Maureen was in the kitchen, poking in the refrigerator.

"Here's my cat, Sharkey," said Alison loudly, setting him down in front of the sofa. She was surprised to see how small he looked on the carpet, since he'd felt so large in her arms.

Dad's eyebrows shot up.

"*Your* cat?" asked Mom.

Maureen, strolling out of the kitchen, gave a snort of disbelief. "You really did bring that funny stray home? Why?"

The white cat stared up at the humans surrounding him. He shrank down against the carpet. His gray ears folded back, and his striped tail sank almost to the floor.

"You're scaring him," said Alison, kneeling on the carpet. "Get back, Maureen."

At the sound of her voice Sharkey turned and gazed into her face. His wide-staring eyes softened, his eyelids drooped meltingly. *Rrr?*

"It's okay, Sharkey," she said.

21

With swift, low-to-the-ground steps Sharkey crept onto Alison's knees, nestling inside her open slicker.

"Look at that," remarked Mr. Harrity. "Love at first bite."

"Just a minute, Alison," said her mother. She looked dismayed. "What gave you the idea it was all right to bring this cat home? I'm sure he belongs to someone—look, he has a collar."

"No, he doesn't belong to anyone." Maureen spoke up, helpful for once. "Mrs. Thompson told Marvin this cat's been hanging around her house for a week, and she really tried to find the owners and couldn't."

"She probably put the collar on herself," added Alison.

"Oh." Mrs. Harrity looked disappointed. "Well then, Alison, what gave you the idea it was all right to bring home any cat? I thought what we agreed was that you could get a kitten, if you still wanted one, after I finish writing my thesis."

"Wrong," said Alison cheerfully. "You said I could get my kitten any time from the Fourth of July on. We put it in writing and we both signed it. Want to see?" Setting Sharkey back on the carpet, she pulled a folded piece of paper out of her slicker pocket.

"Never mind. All right." Mrs. Harrity looked even more dismayed. "I remember now."

Alison's father laughed. "Good for you, Alison. You pinned her down this time."

Alison's mother gave him an unwilling smile. "Easy for you to say, Frank. You go off to work, but I'm right here"—she pointed downward, in the direction of her basement office—"with the cat meowing at the door.

Remember how we let Maureen get a gerbil when she was Alison's age, and I ended up feeding it and cleaning the cage?"

"She wasn't my age," said Alison indignantly. "She was nine. And I'm not Maureen."

Maureen stared haughtily at her mother, as if she had been accused of still sucking her thumb. "I can't believe you're blaming me for something that happened when I was nine."

Alison thought that Maureen would do exactly the same thing if she had a gerbil now, but she didn't want to get into that argument. She had already won the argument she really cared about, she thought, kneeling on the carpet so that Sharkey could climb onto her lap again. She stroked his back and felt the *thrum, thrum* of his purring.

"Sharkey's a weird name," said Maureen. "Why don't you name him something else?"

"But look at his sharp teeth," said Mrs. Harrity, pointing as the cat's pink mouth stretched open in a yawn.

"Of course! And he's white, like the great white shark," said Mr. Harrity with a grin.

"He's Sharkey, that's all," said Alison. Somehow she couldn't imagine calling him anything else.

"He's not *very* white," said her mother. "If you're going to keep him, I hope you'll give him a bath, Alison."

Alison didn't think Sharkey would like a real bath, but she got a damp washcloth and wiped him down. He purred the whole time, rolling over on his back so that she could wipe his belly. But the wiping took quite a while, because the cat kept grabbing the flapping washcloth and tugging it out of her hands.

After Sharkey was three shades whiter and purring quietly on her lap, Alison took a good look at his collar. It was made of something like clear flexible plastic, about as wide as a book-bag strap and as thick as a french fry. Marvin had called it a flea collar, but now she wondered.

The strange thing about the collar was that it didn't have a buckle. Alison turned it around and around, looking for one. How had it gotten over his head in the first place? And if it was a flea collar, why would it have those complicated designs—faint, but Alison could see them—embedded in the clear, thick ring?

Wiggling out of her hands, Sharkey kicked at his collar with a hind paw. He snarled and tried to snap at it, but he couldn't reach. Then he turned to face her. *Meow!*

"I'm sorry," said Alison. "I can't get it off. But how about some dinner?" Leading him to the refrigerator, she took one of the stuffed eggs intended for the Fourth of July cookout tonight at the neighbors' and chopped it up. She'd have Mom buy some regular cat food tomorrow.

Alison watched the way Sharkey ate, crouching over his dish, snapping and gulping without using his paws. Cats were so different from humans. They were *so* different, it was amazing they could be friends. Amazing they could understand each other the way she and Sharkey had, right away.

As Sharkey was licking his saucer clean, Alison's mother came into the kitchen and started pulling dishes out of the refrigerator. "Time to go to the cookout, Alison. Put on a clean pair of jeans, all right?"

"I can't leave Sharkey now," exclaimed Alison. "He'll be lonely."

"Put him in your room," suggested Dad, helping himself to a stuffed egg. "Sharkey'll feel at home there, because it smells like you."

Of course Maureen snickered at the mention of Alison's room smelling, but Alison thought her father might be right. She carried Sharkey into her room and let him sniff around while she changed her jeans and wrote in her diary. She didn't write in it every day, just when something important happened.

July 4

Dear Diary,
I got my new cat! It was like fate. And I can understand everything he tries to tell me.

Alison paused, imagining a *Weekly Informer* headline for her and Sharkey: FREAK OF FATE UNITES GAL WITH KITTY.

There was a light thud as Sharkey landed on the bed beside her. She stroked his back, but he was staring past her at something, twitching his tail. Alison turned to see that he was looking at the stuffed animals on her pillow.

"What do you think, Sharkey? Here's your friend, Curious George." Alison picked up the stuffed monkey's arm and made him wave at Sharkey.

Sharkey leaped sideways high in the air, coming down with all four legs on Curious George. Alison yelped and jerked her hand away.

"Alison, you coming?" her mother called from the hall. "You carry the pasta salad, all right?"

"Coming!" Alison started to lock the strap that fastened the diary shut. Then she remembered that Maureen had an uncanny way of finding the diary and its key, no matter where Alison hid them. She added a PS:

Sharkey is thin but MAUREEN needs to go on a diet.

Alison didn't really think Maureen needed to go on a diet, but she knew that Maureen and her friends worried and talked all the time about whether they did or didn't. Smiling to herself, she pushed the diary under the mattress and replaced the key on top of the door frame.

Then she tiptoed out of the room, leaving Sharkey rolling around on the pillow, clutching Curious George.

·4·

The Mysterious Collar

The next morning, the clouds had cleared and it was warm again. Sharkey, stretched across the foot of Alison's bed, gleamed white in a beam of sunlight. A good day to take him to get his shots, thought Alison as she pulled on her shorts and T-shirt.

Mrs. Harrity wasn't happy about leaving her desk to drive Alison and Sharkey to the vet's, but she admitted it had to be done. At the animal hospital, the vet agreed. "You're smart to protect a nice cat like this," he said as he gave Sharkey his shots. "A little thin, but he'll plump up."

Then the vet fingered the collar around the cat's neck. "Did you put this flea collar on him?" he asked with a frown. "No? Well, let's get rid of it. You should buy him the kind of collar that pulls right off if it catches on a branch or something."

An image of Sharkey choking flashed in Alison's mind, and she felt sick. "But that collar doesn't have any buckle," she said anxiously.

The vet frowned even more as he turned the clear ring around and around, looking for an end. Sharkey kicked at the collar with his hind foot, as if he were trying to help. Finally the vet shrugged and picked up his scissors. "We'll cut it off, then."

But the vet didn't cut the strange collar off Sharkey's neck. He couldn't, although he squeezed the scissor handles until veins bulged in his arm. Sharkey, crouching on the examining table, meowed at being held still so long.

"It's OK, Sharkey. Good boy," said Alison.

"That collar looks like plastic, but it sure doesn't cut like plastic." The vet put his scissors down with a shrug. "Well, I guess he'll be all right with it on. It's not too tight. But you'd better get an ID tag for that collar, a tag with your name and address. You don't want your new cat to get lost."

Sharkey, get lost? Alison felt another wave of anxiety. She hadn't even thought of all the things that might happen to him.

Ordering an ID tag meant another stop, the pet store. "One thing leads to another," grumbled Alison's mother. But as Alison pointed out, they had to stock up on cat food anyway.

Climbing back into the car outside the pet store, Alison felt satisfied. She was doing all the right things to take care of her cat.

But then she looked down at the cardboard cat carrier they'd bought at the vet's and noticed one of Sharkey's white toes, with its pink pad, poking through an air hole. There was something so cute and helpless about that toe. . . . The anxious feeling crept over her

29

again. "What if Sharkey gets lost while I'm waiting for the tag to come?"

"I wouldn't worry about that," said her mother. "Nothing's going to happen to him in just a couple of days."

In fact, a short while later Alison had forgotten all about this worry. Maureen was sick in bed, and Alison got to cat-sit for the Thompsons instead. What luck! she thought, bouncing up the street from her house.

It was all right to be glad Maureen was sick, Alison told herself, because it was just a touch of the flu. And it wasn't as if Maureen were missing anything important. Maureen didn't care about cat-sitting, except for making money.

When Alison had called Marvin to break the news and suggest she could feed the Thompsons' cat, he'd been doubtful. "No, I'd better call someone else. The Thompsons think an eighth grader is taking care of their cat, so—" He had stopped, groaning. "I don't have time. I have to leave to meet Professor Young-man at the lab." So now Alison was skipping over the hill toward the Thompsons' house, swinging their house key from its loop of string.

In the stuffy, lukewarm air of the Thompsons' shut-up house, Alison didn't see the black Persian cat. She checked the living room and dining room, calling, "Here, kitty, kitty."

Then she spotted the cat in the kitchen. Black Beauty was crouching on top of the toaster oven, under a cupboard. The fluffy black cat stared past Alison with wide pupils, her tongue sticking out a little and her ears and whiskers twitching in different directions.

Alison gasped. "What's the matter, Black Beauty?" She put her hand out, then pulled it back. Was the cat being electrocuted by the toaster oven? She thought she saw something sparkling in the deep black ruff around the cat's neck.

Now Black Beauty's face had stopped twitching, but her shoulders gave a single jerk. Her ears folded back and she growled, staring into space. Maybe the toaster oven had nothing to do with it, Alison thought. The sparkling was probably one of those jeweled collars they sold in the pet store.

Was the cat having some kind of fit? Alison wondered if, as cat-sitter, she would have to take Black Beauty to the vet's.

Then Black Beauty gave a low yowl and shook herself all over. Crawling out from under the cupboard, she sniffed Alison's hand daintily.

"Are you okay? Nice Black Beauty. Pretty kitty." Alison started to rub behind the cat's ears, but Black Beauty jumped down to the floor. Looking from her food dish to Alison, she meowed.

"Okay, I get it," said Alison. The stack of cat food cans was on the counter, just where Marvin had said it would be. Alison selected a can of Princess Kitty Gourmet Choice, chicken à la king flavor, and pulled the lid off by the ring.

Black Beauty meowed and meowed until Alison had spooned the food into her dish.

"There you go," said Alison, smoothing the cat's silky fur as she began to eat.

But the minute Alison lifted her hand, Black Beauty stopped eating and meowed again. "You want me to pet you while you're eating?" Alison could hardly believe this; she wouldn't have wanted it herself. But the black Persian refused to eat unless Alison kept stroking her.

"You just want attention," said Alison, but she didn't mind. After all, Black Beauty had the loveliest soft fur. Especially the long ruff around her neck, Alison thought, as she sank her fingers into it.

But just a minute. There was something firm and slick under Black Beauty's ruff. Some kind of strap—a collar. Pushing back the silky black fur, Alison expected to see a rhinestone collar. It *was* a collar, but not one with rhinestones. Just a plain band of clear plastic.

Or was it plain? The light in the corner of the kitchen was dim, and Alison bent over the cat to see. There were curlicues and swirls embedded in the collar. And when Alison turned it around, she was not really surprised to find that it had no buckle.

The collar was exactly like Sharkey's.

For a moment Alison was afraid, and the emptiness of the Thompsons' house suddenly seemed creepy. Then she shook her head, annoyed at herself. Why should she think there was anything mysterious about the collars just because she hadn't noticed this kind before? Probably if she went back to the pet store, she'd see them hanging on the rack, right next to the jeweled ones.

Besides, there was something to be glad about. If Sharkey and Black Beauty had the same kind of collar, that meant the Thompsons *must* have put Sharkey's collar on him. So when the Thompsons came home, they'd explain how to take it off, and Alison could get him the kind the vet had recommended. Even more important, Alison didn't have to worry about an owner wanting Sharkey back.

·5·

The Weekly Informer

As Alison stepped onto the sidewalk in front of the 7-Eleven store, the digital clock on the bank across the street showed one o'clock exactly. Where was Denise? She always got snippy if *she* had to wait.

To get out of the muggy sunshine, Alison squeezed into the narrow band of shade cast by the roof of the 7-Eleven. It was an uncomfortable way to wait. Besides, she was eager to tell Denise about her cat-sitting job. And if Denise didn't come right away, they wouldn't have much time for secret reading before Alison had to leave for chess.

Alison's mind had drifted from chess class, to the Living Chess game the fifth graders put on last year, to how funny Denise had looked, in white makeup, as the White Queen, when Denise herself appeared on the other side of the street.

Alison wondered if the reason Denise was late had anything to do with the strange way she was walking. Facing forward, but with her body turned sideways

and her arms held out, Denise was doing some complicated kind of step. It took her forward along the sidewalk, ending in a kick, and then back again in the same way.

"What's the matter with you?" Alison shouted across the street, suspecting that Denise knew she was watching her. In fact, Denise seemed to *want* Alison to watch.

Sure enough, Denise did a few more dance steps before she looked both ways and ran across to the 7-Eleven. "Jazz dancing is so much fun you wouldn't believe it!" she panted. "It's too bad you didn't sign up. The teacher shows you how to really get in touch with your body, so you can make different parts go different ways."

"Different parts go different ways?" It reminded Alison of the way Black Beauty's ears and whiskers had twitched. "I'm glad I'm taking chess. It sharpens your mind."

Denise only gave Alison a pitying look. Alison remembered, with a flash of anger, what Sonia had said about geeks taking chess. With an effort she pulled herself away from the argument she and Denise were sliding into. "Anyway, let's go buy the *Weekly Informer.*" She stepped into the air-conditioned cool of the store.

"*And* candy," said Denise, following Alison. "Remember, all we have left in the secret hoard is those stale gumdrops."

"The gumdrops aren't so bad," said Alison, who was saving up to pay for Sharkey's ID tag. She picked up a copy of the *Weekly Informer* from the top of the stack. There was her story, ALIEN PLANT MUNCHES MAILMAN, with a photograph of a jungly vine draped over a mailbox.

Alison felt a pleasant tickle of horror and excitement. Of course she didn't really believe that a plant—even an alien plant—had eaten a mailman. But there was something delicious about the way the *Weekly Informer* told these stories, as if they were absolutely true.

The top story was the one Denise wanted: FORMER MISS AMERICA'S SEARING SECRET. The headline was almost two inches high. The picture beside the headline showed a young woman in a tight sequined dress, shielding her face with one long-nailed hand. Denise, peering over Alison's shoulder, sighed happily.

"You planning to buy that paper, kids?" The sharp voice of the 7-Eleven clerk made both girls jump. Alison put the *Weekly Informer* on the counter, and Denise put a dollar bill on top of it. "We'd like that in a bag, please," Denise told the clerk.

"Uh-huh," said the woman, dropping the tabloid into a paper bag.

Alison blushed and hurried out of the store ahead of Denise. Did the 7-Eleven clerk guess that the girls carried the *Weekly Informer* in a bag so no one would know they read it? They'd started asking for a bag after Denise's mother had taken a *Weekly Informer* away from Denise, calling it "unsavory reading material." "Unsavory" seemed to mean shocking or disgusting, but fascinating at the same time.

"Remember, I've got dibs on FORMER MISS AMERICA'S SEARING SECRET." Denise pulled the paper out of the bag and stopped on the curb to read the front-page headlines again. Taking a pink felt pen from her pocket, she marked her choice.

"Fine," said Alison, looking over Denise's shoulder. "I've got dibs on ALIEN PLANT—"

Alison stopped short, her eyes resting on the third and smallest headline, MY CAT SOLD OUT TO THE IRS! And a smaller subhead, PSYCHIC EXPERT UNCOVERS IRS PET-NAPPING.

The IRS? For a moment Alison didn't know what that meant, and then she remembered. Last April, when it was time for Mom and Dad to pay their income taxes, it seemed every other word they said was "I-R-S." The way they said it, "IRS" sounded like a swearword, but it was just the part of the government you paid income taxes to.

But what could the IRS possibly want with cats? Alison had to find out. "Dibs on MY CAT SOLD OUT TO THE IRS!" she finished.

Denise gave Alison a grown-up little smile, as if to say, I knew you'd pick one like that. She replaced the pink felt pen in her pocket, took out a yellow one, and marked Alison's headline. "Okay. As long as yours isn't on the same page as mine."

"You don't have to mark our stories," said Alison. "There's only two of us, and we're not going to forget which ones we picked. And what does it matter if they're on the same page?" she went on as they crossed the street.

"Don't you remember," said Denise, "in the Candy Club Rules for Secret Reading, Rule Number 2? 'Take turns choosing stories to read. If your favorite story is on the same page as someone else's, you have to give it to them as soon as you finish the story you chose. No fair reading other—' "

"Yeah, yeah," said Alison. Denise had written out twelve rules, neatly spaced, in her careful, tiny handwriting, and they kept them with their stash of secret reading in Alison's room. But Alison had never read the rules all the way through.

As the girls began the steep, winding walk up Chestnut Hill Road, Denise spoke in a casual tone. "You know, I've been thinking. Maybe we should invite more kids into the club."

"Why?" asked Alison in surprise. She had thought Denise felt the same way she did—that the club was the most fun with just the two of them.

"Well, we could do more things. More mature activities."

Alison gave her friend a puzzled glance. "More mature?" There was that word Sonia had used at the parade, and Denise had started using only a couple of days ago. "More mature activities, like what?"

"Oh, maybe like trying different hairstyles and learning how to use hair spray. Or—" Denise looked up into the leafy horse-chestnut trees, as if she were having a splendid vision. "Or like a beauty pageant."

Alison stared at her friend's round face, at her glasses and her limp straw-colored hair. "I don't think they'd let us enter a beauty pageant," she said finally,

39

as they rounded the last curve before Alison's driveway.

"Not someone else's beauty pageant." Denise smiled patiently. "I mean, we'd do our own. It would help us develop poise and a sense of style."

"Oh, you mean do it by ourselves without anyone watching." For a moment, Alison had thought Denise was losing her marbles. She was certainly talking in an odd way.

As Alison opened the side door of her house, she spotted Maureen on the family-room sofa. She motioned to Denise to keep the bag out of sight. Ever since Denise's mother had discovered her "unsavory" reading material, the girls had done their secret reading at Alison's house. But Alison didn't want her family to find the *Weekly Informer*s either. Her parents might not take them away from her, but they'd certainly laugh. Maureen would be the worst—she'd go on teasing for days.

"Hey," said Alison to her sister, "I thought Mom told you no TV during the day."

Maureen shrugged. "There's nothing else to do. I'm not that sick anymore, but she won't let me have anyone over."

R-row? It was Sharkey, running into the kitchen. He put his white front paws up on Alison's knees and lifted his chin to be scratched.

"Maybe he's not such a bad mascot," remarked Denise as they hurried through the hall to Alison's room. She put down the bag and tried to pick the cat up. "Nice kitty." But Sharkey's eyes widened in alarm, and he struggled out of Denise's hands.

40

"I guess he doesn't really like to be picked up by anyone but me." Alison tried to sound apologetic, but secretly she was pleased. "My father went to the store last night and got Sharkey a catnip mouse. Sharkey played with it, but he still wouldn't let Dad pick him up."

"The mascot of a club should like everyone in the club," said Denise. She shut the door of Alison's room and locked it. "Oh, well. You missed your chance to get that orange kitten. Let's start."

· 6 ·

Secret Reading

In silence, in case Maureen was listening outside the door, the two girls began the preparations for their meeting. Alison pulled her diary out from under her mattress, and Denise took the diary key from its hiding place, the top of the door frame. Then Alison unlocked her diary and opened the secret compartment at the back. It contained five flattened gumdrops.

Using the diary key, Denise sliced one gumdrop exactly in half. The girls took turns choosing gumdrops until they each had two and a half. Then they settled themselves comfortably on Alison's bed, and Sharkey settled himself comfortably on Alison's lap.

It was good to have a fresh new *Weekly Informer* to read. At their last secret reading meeting, Denise and Alison had gotten out the pile of old tabloids they kept hidden under Alison's rug. They'd already read all the stories, so they read the ads: "Mystical Talisman Grants Your Every Wish ($7.95 postpaid)" and "Genuine Diamond Ring for Only $1." Denise had tried to talk Alison into chipping in to buy the diamond ring, but Alison was sure they'd get cheated. Anyhow, she didn't want a diamond ring as much as Denise did.

"Let's see what pages the stories we chose are on." Denise took the *Weekly Informer* from the bag and flipped through it. "They always hide the best stories in the middle, so you can't just read them in the store and not buy the paper. Oh, good, this works out. FORMER MISS AMERICA is on page eighteen, and your story about cats is on page forty-seven."

Alison took her part of the paper from Denise, bent over a picture—and almost choked on her hard pink gumdrop. The caption was "High-Tech Collar Turns Tabby into Traitor." The photograph showed a wide-eyed tiger cat, with its tongue sticking out, wearing a familiar-looking collar. The headline on this page shouted, IRS TO BLAME IN CAT-OWNER'S ORDEAL.

According to the story, a man in Shrewsbury—a town not far from Alison's—had noticed something strange about his cat, Ethel. She came home one day wearing a collar he couldn't get off. "And all of a sudden, she'd sit staring into space with her tongue sticking out and her ears and whiskers twitching," said Ethel's owner.

A creepy feeling was seeping down Alison's spine. The same feeling that had come over her when she discovered Black Beauty's collar.

Nervously Alison popped her second gumdrop, a green one, into her mouth. As she read on, she soothed herself by rubbing Sharkey's ears.

43

"I didn't suspect the IRS at first," said the Shrewsbury man. "Why should I? I pay my taxes." Then he saw an "expert" on a TV talk show—a psychic who specialized in pet problems. The cat owner rushed to the psychic, who explained everything: "The government is developing high-tech pet collars. If these gadgets work, they'll force cats and dogs to report tax-dodging owners to government snoops. The IRS hopes to find thousands of tax cheats by making Fido and Tabby spy on their unsuspecting owners!"

Alison drew in her breath sharply. Could the Thompsons be tax dodgers? The IRS must think so, or why would they collar both the cats—Black Beauty and Sharkey—at their house?

At a squeal from Denise, Alison looked up, annoyed. Sharkey had pounced on Denise's last gumdrop and was batting it across the bedspread like a soccer player going for a goal. "No!" Alison told him, snatching the gumdrop from between his white paws. It was yellow, Denise's favorite kind.

Alison brushed the gumdrop off on her T-shirt and handed it back to Denise. "Sorry." To Sharkey she said, "Here, you can play with the monkey." She held out Curious George, making his legs wiggle.

"It's not very sanitary to have a pet on your bed while we're eating," said Denise, but she popped the gumdrop into her mouth. "You should have put him out, Alison."

"Oh, big deal," said Alison. "He didn't bite the gumdrop or anything. But listen, Denise." Alison leaned across the bedspread toward her friend. "There's something weird going on. See this collar on Sharkey? It doesn't have any buckle, and the vet couldn't cut it off no matter how hard he tried. And Black Beauty has the same kind of collar, and so does the cat in this picture, it looks like. Well, why would the Thompsons have two cats with these collars at their house, unless they hadn't paid their taxes, and the IRS—" Realizing that Denise was staring at her with an uneasy expression, Alison stopped.

"What are you talking about?" asked Denise. "You don't really think that cat"—she pointed to the picture in the paper—"was spying for the IRS, do you?"

Alison felt her face grow warm. "I know it sounds crazy. But you should have seen the way the Thompsons' cat was acting today. So weird! And she's wearing *exactly* the same kind of collar as Sharkey."

Denise licked the tip of her forefinger and pressed it into the secret compartment, picking up the last crumbs of gumdrop sugar. She didn't look at Alison as she licked the sugar off her finger and spoke again. "I wish you'd stop this pretending. It was all right when we were still in the fifth grade, but now . . . I don't know if I can talk Sonia into joining."

"*What?*" It was Alison's turn to stare at her friend as if she were crazy. "Talk Sonia into joining what?" But Alison knew the answer. She felt breathless, as if she had just fallen into a cold swimming pool.

Denise gave Alison a sudden determined look. "I think I could get Sonia to join our club, if we were doing more mature activities. Okay, you don't know her that well, but I'm telling you, she's going to be one of the most popular kids in the sixth grade. You saw her on the float, with those boys yelling at her."

"I don't know that many kids who like her," protested Alison. The cold swimming pool seemed to have turned into a fast-flowing stream, carrying her along in a direction she didn't want to go.

"That doesn't matter," said Denise in the tone of a teacher explaining for the tenth time how to multiply fractions. "As soon as we get to the intermediate school, everyone's going to see how mature she is. Sonia told me she's practically sure this seventh-grade boy is going to ask her out." Denise paused to let that sink in. "Anyway, we need more kids to do a beauty pageant, and Sonia's good at dancing and makeup and wearing the right outfits."

"Maybe I don't want to do a beauty pageant," muttered Alison. She picked up Sharkey and hugged him to her. He purred loudly, kneading her arm.

"It'll be lots of fun! Alison, you'll like it." Denise put on her most winning expression. "You've already got the perfect thing for your interview."

"Interview?"

"In the pageant." Denise looked as if Alison wasn't catching on very fast. "Beauty pageants aren't just about looks, you know. You have to have a talent, like jazz dancing, and you have to show your personality, like how you love animals and rescued a stray kitten, in the interview."

"Oh." That sounded a little bit better. "I guess I could tell how I play chess and won the fifth-grade tournament, too." Alison stared thoughtfully past her friend. Denise knew the whole story, even the part Alison would never tell in a beauty pageant.

Who would believe that Marvin Smith had invented a machine, a magical machine that really worked, to help her win the chess tournament? That machine (he called it the DISAST) had gotten her into so much trouble, at school and at home. Finally, the DISAST had almost lost her the tournament—and all her friends.

Alison realized she was looking at her alarm clock, and it was 2:45. "Chess! I have to leave for chess."

Hurriedly she locked her diary, pushed it back under the mattress, and hid the key. Denise folded up the *Weekly Informer* very neatly, squirmed under the bed, and slid the paper under the rug next to the older issues. She squirmed out again, sneezing, with dust balls on the front of her T-shirt. "Ugh! Doesn't your mother ever vacuum under the bed?"

"No," said Alison pointedly. "That's why we decided to hide the papers at my house, remember? Your mother cleans up too much."

On her bike, sailing through the thick, warm air down the curves of Chestnut Hill Road, Alison bit her lip in embarrassment. Why, why had she said anything to Denise about the cats and their collars? She'd gotten carried away all right, taking one of those stories in the *Weekly Informer* seriously.

The collar on the cat in the *Weekly Informer,* as well as Sharkey's and Black Beauty's collars, must be just some kind of flea collar. And obviously the Thompsons must have put Sharkey's collar on him—

she'd already figured that out. They were supposed to come home from their trip this afternoon, weren't they? Alison would walk over there later and ask them how to get the collar off.

As she pushed her bike into a rack at the intermediate school, Alison noticed that the building seemed different. In September, this wouldn't be just the place where the summer classes were held. It would be Alison's school. Denise's school.

And, unfortunately, Sonia's school. Last year Sonia had made a big deal about how "weak" fifth-grade boys were and how she couldn't wait for sixth grade, which meant intermediate school with all those cute seventh- and eighth-grade boys. And she'd gone around talking about the "right clothes" and making fun of anyone who wore things that weren't in style. A lot of kids didn't like her for that. But maybe Sonia would be ready for sixth grade—and Alison wouldn't.

To get away from her disturbing thoughts, Alison hurried into the building and followed the signs to intermediate chess. It was a relief to sit down in the chalk-smelling classroom and bend over a chessboard. Playing chess was like stepping into another world. On the dark and light squares, there were no worrisome cat collars, no Sonia with her "mature" ways. Only the board, the pieces, and the moves of the game.

·7·

Collar Trouble

Sharkey was waiting inside the back door when Alison got home. *R-row?* Alison picked him up and stroked him, but her attention was more on her sister. Maureen was strolling from the hall into the kitchen with a very, very casual expression on her face.

"Have a nice chess class?" she asked, crossing the family room to turn on the TV.

"You were snooping in my room again, weren't you?" said Alison.

Her sister flung her a look of pained amusement. "Your room really isn't as incredibly interesting as you think, Alison."

"You were snooping, I can tell."

Alison was about to point out the dust ball clinging to one leg of Maureen's shorts when the doorbell rang. Alison went to the side door, still holding Sharkey.

It was Marvin. "We almost didn't get paid," he growled at Alison. "Mrs. Thompson thought we were

49

fooling around with her cat. Did you put that collar on Black Beauty?"

Maureen, listening from the sofa, giggled. "Haven't you heard? The government kidnapped the cat and put the collar on."

"You did snoop, you jerk!" exclaimed Alison. To Marvin she answered, "Me? Put a collar on the Thompsons' cat?" She paused, trying to catch hold of her scrambling thoughts. "Just a minute. The Thompsons thought *I* put their cat's collar on? But you told me they put Sharkey's collar on. But they couldn't have, if they're mad about . . . And you know what?"

"What?" Marvin was waiting with his arms folded.

Alison hesitated, wondering if she should tell Marvin about the *Weekly Informer* story. On the one hand, he was an eighth-grade boy. On the other hand, Marvin was interested in weird science-fiction kinds of things. He'd even made a weird science-fiction thing happen last spring, when he invented that machine to help Alison win chess games.

She had to tell him. "Listen, I know this sounds weird, but somebody's going around putting these collars on cats. The cat in the *Weekly Informer* had one, and so does Sharkey. Exactly like Black Beauty's. See? And Black Beauty had the same kind of fit as that cat Ethel."

Marvin stared at Sharkey's neck for a moment, turning the collar around with one finger. Then he said grimly, "I should have known better than to let a fifth grader take over my job. Why'd you do a stupid thing like that?"

"But I didn't!" Alison sputtered. Marvin had completely misunderstood.

"No, no, you've got it all wrong, Marvin." Maureen, between bubbles of laughter, pretended to be explaining for her younger sister. "The IRS put the collars on both the cats."

"It'd serve you right if I didn't give you your cut," said Marvin to Alison. As he pulled bills and coins from his shorts pocket and counted the money into Alison's hand, he turned his scowl on Maureen. "That stuff about the government isn't funny. If you'd done the job yourself, like you said—"

"I'm not being funny," said Maureen with a smirk. "You should read this article in Alison's *Weekly Informer*. MY CAT SOLD OUT TO THE IRS! That cat had a collar on, too, so that proves it." She gave a scornful laugh. "You are so gullible, Alison. You'd probably believe it if they said aliens from outer space put the collars on."

"Oh, shut up, Maureen." Alison wished she could stuff a sofa cushion into Maureen's laughing mouth. To Marvin she pleaded, "I did *not*—"

Marvin, on his way out the door, frowned and waved his hand. "Never mind, the job's over. But if you want to make up for it, you should go tell Mrs. Thompson how to get the collar off. That's what upset her the most."

As the screen door shut behind Marvin, Alison turned back toward the family room. Maureen, lounging on the sofa, was pretending to be absorbed in a talk show. "You have *no right* . . ." Alison began.

Then, seeing Sharkey's ears flatten at her sharp tone of voice, she stopped. Turning on her heel, she carried Sharkey to her room to put her money away.

By dinnertime Alison was still mad at Maureen, but she couldn't figure out how to avoid eating with her. If Alison tried to explain why she didn't feel like eating at the same table as her sister, Mom and Dad would find out that Alison had been reading (and maybe believing) the *Weekly Informer.*

Alison decided to just ignore Maureen and look past her at Sharkey, who was crouching on the back of the armchair facing the family room. He watched the humans closely, licking his lips each time one of them lifted a chicken leg for a bite. When he saw Alison pull off a scrap of gristle and put her hand under the table, he jumped down to grab the scrap.

"I didn't know it was all right to feed the cat at the table," said Maureen.

"Don't give him any more," Mom told Alison. "Didn't you already feed him his dinner? You can give him scraps after we finish." She turned to frown at Maureen's plate. "Are you still feeling sick? You didn't take any rice salad. And only one little drumstick?"

"I'm not that hungry," said Maureen. But Alison saw her look longingly at the chicken platter and then away again.

Digging into the rice salad, Alison smiled to herself. Maureen must have read her diary when she snooped this afternoon. If Alison's diet remark had Maureen worried about her weight, it served her right. Especially after she'd told on Alison for feeding Sharkey at the table.

As Sharkey jumped back up to his perch on the armchair, Alison reached for a second drumstick. Then she stopped with her hand halfway to the platter. What was that light coming from Sharkey's neck? His collar. Sparkling!

Alison leaped to her feet. The lights inside the collar were dancing in a rapid pattern.

"Alison!" Her mother sounded annoyed, but in the next breath she exclaimed, "What's the matter with Sharkey?"

"Ee-yew, his tongue's sticking out," said Maureen.

"Stay away from the cat," Dad snapped at Alison. "He's having some kind of fit."

But Alison paid no attention to any of them. She bent over the armchair, stroking Sharkey. "Poor baby! What's the matter? Poor kitty, are you okay?"

Although his collar had stopped sparkling, Sharkey didn't seem okay. His tongue was sticking out, and his whiskers and ears were twitching in different directions. Oh, no, thought Alison. Just like the Thompsons' cat. Just like the cat in the *Weekly Informer.*

Alison tried to pick Sharkey up, but his claws were sunk deep into the upholstery. He let out a yowl. Her father pulled her backward by her elbows. "Didn't you hear me? We don't know what's the matter with him."

"Yes I do!" It had come suddenly clear in Alison's mind, the way chess moves sometimes appeared to her on the board. "It's his collar! It's doing something to him, sparkling. We *have* to get that collar off of him."

Alison gasped for breath. "See, the Thompsons' cat has the same kind of collar, and I thought they put Sharkey's collar on him, but they think I put Black Beauty's collar on *her*—"

"But really the government did it," broke in Maureen's mock-earnest voice. "It tells all about it in Alison's *Weekly Informer.* The Internal Revenue Service thinks you guys cheated on your income taxes, so they put this high-tech collar on Sharkey, so he could spy on—"

"That's a cheap shot, Maureen," snapped their mother. "Teasing Alison when she's upset about her cat." She got up and put an arm around Alison. "We're worried about Sharkey, too. I'll call the vet if he gets worse. But look, he seems all right now."

Sharkey was sitting up straight, perfectly calm. He gazed at the humans around him as if they had been the ones acting odd. Licking one paw, he rubbed it over his ear.

"But it was the collar," said Alison urgently. "I saw it sparkling just before he started having the fit."

Her parents exchanged glances. "You read something in a tabloid, the *Weekly Informer,* about the IRS spying on people through cats?" asked Dad. "That *taxes* the imagination." He chuckled at his own joke, then went on in a gentle tone. "You can't believe what you read in those papers, pumpkin."

Pumpkin, her baby nickname. Alison felt her face grow hot. "I know that! But Sharkey's collar was sparkling, just the way Black Beauty's collar did when she was acting weird this morning. She looked just like Sharkey did."

"Sharkey might have caught something from the Thompsons' cat," suggested her mother. "I'll call the vet in the morning."

Dad nodded, examining Sharkey's collar. "See how the kitchen light shines off the plastic? That's what you saw, Alison. There's nothing in the collar, like a battery, that could have produced sparks."

Alison felt like screaming. No one believed her. She was the only one who had seen the dancing lights in the collars. She was the only one who knew how the real cats' collars fit in with the story in the *Weekly Informer.*

As they all sat down again, the telephone rang. Maureen got up to answer it. "Marvin," she said, holding out the phone to Alison.

Alison took it hopefully. Had Marvin changed his mind about letting her help with his cat-sitting business?

Clearing his throat in an embarrassed way, Marvin spoke. "Uh . . . you still got that article?"

"Article?"

"Yeah, about"—Marvin lowered his voice—"somebody putting weird collars on cats?"

"Oh, you mean the one in—" Alison glanced over at her family sitting around the kitchen table. Alison's sister, helping herself to rice salad at last, had that casual look on her face that meant she was paying too much attention. "I know what you mean."

"Well, I want to look at it. Because there's something fishy going on here." Marvin paused. "Don't tell Maureen about this, but all four of the cats I'm sitting for—now they all have those collars."

·*8*·

CodeCracking

Alison's heart lifted. Marvin believed—no, Marvin *knew*—that mysterious collars were mysteriously appearing on cats. "Well, do you think the government—" Alison paused, glancing back at Maureen. Her sister was pretending to study an olive in her rice salad, but Alison was sure she was listening with ears as sharp as Sharkey's. "Who do you think did it?"

"Yeah, that's the question, all right," answered Marvin. "After I've read that article, I'll formulate a hypothesis."

"A what?"

"A hypothesis. You know, a sort of working idea of how the collars operate and so on. Then I'll take one of those cats to my house and test out the hypothesis."

"But wait a minute." Alison's mind was racing. If Marvin found out how the collars operated, he'd find out how to take them off. "Why don't you just test the thing on Sharkey?"

"No, I have to do it here, because I'm using my computer."

"*We* have a computer!" exclaimed Alison. Of course she meant Mom's computer in the basement, the one she was writing her thesis on. As soon as she'd said the words, Alison knew she was heading for trouble. She knew she'd better add, "But I don't know if Mom would let us use it."

But before Alison could speak, Marvin said, "You do? That would work out. That would be better, in fact," he added thoughtfully. "If I borrowed one of my neighbors' cats, they might find out and—well, it would just be better not to. So anyway, I'll come by in a few minutes."

What luck! Marvin Smith, the science genius, was now on the case. Marvin was what the *Weekly Informer* liked to call an "expert." On the other hand . . . Alison was not comfortable about the plan to use her mother's computer.

Fortunately, her mother and father were out of the house on one of their long evening walks by the time Marvin showed up. A computer disk and a coil of wire in one hand, Marvin stepped briskly into the kitchen.

"Hi, Maureen." He waved to Alison's sister, on the phone with one of her friends. Taking the *Weekly Informer* from Alison, he read it on the way down the basement stairs. Alison followed, carrying Sharkey.

"That's the collar, all right," muttered Marvin as he read. "And that's the same kind of fit this cat I'm cat-

58

sitting had. But 'psychic expert'—what a bunch of baloney. You said you saw Black Beauty with her tongue sticking out and so on?"

"And Sharkey had a fit tonight, too." It was cool in the basement, and Alison, with only shorts and a T-shirt on, shivered. She switched on the light in her mother's office. "Here's the computer. But be really careful, because this is where my mother's writing her thesis, and . . ."

Marvin was paying no attention. "Good, this is a PC like mine." Dropping the paper on Mrs. Harrity's desk, he flipped switches and twirled knobs. The computer woke up with a groan.

"What about Sharkey's collar?" asked Alison, remembering the reason she was taking this risk. She sat down in her mother's chair and held the cat on her lap while Marvin carefully examined the thick, clear ring around Sharkey's neck.

"Yeah, the same collar. I should have realized before, this is advanced technology. I bet the IRS got it from the Navy. From that program to use dolphins against enemy subs."

What Marvin was saying frightened Alison, but at the same time she was glad he seemed to know so much about it. "What is the part that sparkles? Those patterns that you can hardly see?"

Marvin nodded. "I think it's a super-miniaturized radiolike device with an encoding and decoding function." As he spoke, Marvin slipped his disk into the disk drive and leaned behind the computer to connect the coil of wire he'd brought.

59

"I don't know if you should fiddle around with that part," said Alison uneasily.

"I won't hurt anything," said Marvin absently. "And I have to hook up the collar to the program—that's the whole point."

"But what are you *doing?*" demanded Alison. "What does the computer have to do with the collars?"

Marvin stopped with the wire half uncoiled, looked at Alison, and sighed. "All right, I'll explain." He shook his head and sighed again. "But it's so hard to make it simple enough for you to understand. Okay, here's my hypothesis. Say that someone is kidnapping Sharkey and the other cats and putting these collars on them."

"The IRS," said Alison.

"The IRS, or anyone with advanced technology," agreed Marvin. "Anyway, say the patterns in the collars are like the circuitry in a transistor radio. Say that what the collars do is send commands from the 'anyone' to Sharkey. That's probably what those fits are, when the cats get the messages."

"That's why they twitch?" asked Alison in horror. "Because they're getting shocks?"

"I wouldn't call them *shocks,*" said Marvin. "Just electrical impulses. In order to reach his brain"—Marvin gestured at the cat's gray-striped head—"the messages would have to be in electrical impulses."

Alison shook her head, puzzled. "Why would they?"

"Because that's the way thoughts travel in the brain: electrical impulses." Marvin's expression said that everyone should know that. "Anyway, obviously whoever put the collar on isn't going to think in the same elec-

60

trical code as Sharkey. So the collar, besides receiving the message, has to translate it into—well, you might say, into cat language."

"Cat language?" Alison wondered if she'd made a mistake, asking Marvin for help. Marvin was very smart, but he also had some very weird ideas.

Marvin rolled his eyes upward and remarked to himself, "Professor Youngman warned me. The most difficult part of scientific work is explaining it to people with no scientific background." To Alison he said, "Forget about 'cat language.' I was just trying to explain it in words you could understand. This problem really has to do with encoding and decoding."

Alison was about to ask him what that meant when she realized they had just been through this. And Mom and Dad weren't going to stay out on their walk forever. She nodded as if she understood. "Okay."

"Okay," agreed Marvin. Uncoiling the rest of the wire, he held out the two ends like suction cups toward the cat. "Hold him still."

"No!" exclaimed Alison. Sharkey bolted from her lap and leaped up on top of the computer.

Marvin dropped his hands back. "What's your problem? It was your idea to use Sharkey."

"Sorry," muttered Alison. "I want to know what you're going to do to him first."

"Nothing. Jeez!" Marvin snorted. "I mean, I'm just going to attach electrodes to his collar so I can run his thought impulses through CodeCracker. That's a computer program to decode messages," he added as Alison's mouth opened for another question. "See, the device in the collar would translate the messages they're sending into a code Sharkey would understand. But it wouldn't translate them into English, so I have to prepare the program to do that. But Sharkey won't feel a thing." He pressed one electrode to each side of his own head. "See how much it hurts?"

"Sorry," said Alison again. She was watching Sharkey, who was peering down at the screen with his gray ears pricked forward. For the first time, Alison noticed what the screen said: CodeCracker, and a copyright date.

"He's okay up there," said Marvin, picking up the wire with the suction cups again. "Just hold him still while I put the electrodes on his collar."

Alison stood beside the computer table and put an arm around Sharkey. As she rubbed under his chin and around his ears, she kept a close eye on what Marvin was doing. But Marvin only taped the electrodes to the collar, as he'd said. Sharkey tried to nip at the wire, but Alison held him close and gently rumpled his ears. The cat purred, closing his eyes.

"Okay," muttered Marvin. Sitting down in front of the computer, he began tapping the keys. With his monkeylike face intent on the screen and his wiry body hunched over the keyboard, he looked like an illustration for a book called *Curious George and His PC*.

Alison kept her hands on Sharkey in case he suddenly decided to jump down. She couldn't see the screen very well from where she was standing. "What're you doing?" she asked.

"I'm not sure, to tell you the truth." Marvin didn't look up from the screen. "I had to modify this program to accept the thought impulses from the electrodes, and it may not work at all."

"But I mean, if it does work, what will happen?"

Marvin didn't answer. His eyes were widening, and he tapped furiously. "Entered," he breathed, staring from the screen to Sharkey and back again.

"What?" demanded Alison. But Marvin, a smile spreading across his face, still didn't answer. Alison leaned over as far as she could and managed to read the white letters lining up on the dark screen: NICE . . . NICE . . . NICE . . . Marvin half stood and put his hand on the cat's back. "That's his purr," he whispered.

Alison caught her breath in delight. The words were appearing exactly in the rhythm of Sharkey's purr.

For a few moments they watched in silence. Alison had never seen Marvin look so pleased with himself. Then Alison asked, "Isn't there any more than that?"

"He must have more thoughts than that, or how could he receive messages?" Marvin gazed thoughtfully at Sharkey's flat little head. "Stop petting him. Let's try to get him to think about something else."

Alison took her hands off the cat. He purred on for a few moments, filling the screen with lines of NICE . . . NICE . . . NICE. Then he sat up and gazed around the room. His yellow eyes focused on a point high on the paneled wall.

"He's looking at something up there," said Alison. "What is that dark spot?"

63

Marvin, tapping at the keyboard, pointed to the screen:

MOTH: POUNCE / PLAY / EAT   YUM—YUM

"Yuck, Sharkey," said Alison. "You like moths?"

"Let's see what he thinks of this," said Marvin. He plucked a pencil from the pencil mug on the desk and wiggled the eraser end over the top of the computer.

Staring intently, Sharkey shot a paw out and hooked the eraser. The screen showed WIGGLY WIGGLY GOTCHA.

"Yeah, baby!" Dropping the pencil, Marvin flicked his fingers over the keyboard. "There, that's entered. Now, if we could just make him mad about something. . . ."

"He hates the collar," suggested Alison. She gave the clear ring around his neck a tug. "Sharkey, look at your collar."

Sharkey twisted his head and tried to snap at the collar, although he couldn't reach it. Marvin laughed out loud, nodding at the screen as he tapped keys. MOUSE—DUNG COLLAR, the white letters said.

Alison laughed, too. But then a familiar sound upstairs made her gasp. "Mom and Dad. They're back. Oh, no. She's opening the basement door! Stop right now."

Marvin jumped up, working quickly and coolly to unfasten Sharkey and hand him to Alison, then disconnect the wire from the computer, pull the program from the computer, and turn the computer off. He slipped his program disk and the coiled wire into his shorts pocket just a second before Mrs. Harrity appeared in the doorway.

"Marvin. Alison. I *thought* I saw a light on. What are you doing down here?"

"I was just showing Marvin your office," said Alison. She hoped Mom wouldn't notice how high and strained her voice was.

"Yeah, I'll be writing a Ph.D. thesis myself someday," said Marvin in a hearty tone. "Just wanted to see where you do your work."

With a suspicious glance, Alison's mother put her hand on the computer. "It's warm," she said. "As if someone had just been using it."

"Sharkey," said Alison quickly. "I mean," she explained as her mother raised her eyebrows, "he was sitting on top of it."

"The next time Sharkey wants to use the computer," said Mrs. Harrity, "just to sit on, of course—he'd better ask."

Alison felt like a jerk, but Marvin didn't seem bothered at all. As they climbed the stairs, he whispered over his shoulder to Alison. "Bring him to my house tomorrow. We're on their tail now!"

·*9*·

Not Pretending

Alison woke up the next morning to find Sharkey sitting on top of her. When he saw her open her eyes, he began purring and kneading her stomach with his white paws. Alison seemed to hear his thoughts come out with the *thrum . . . thrum* of his purr: N I C E . . . N I C E . . . Then she remembered something very important, something that had slipped her mind last night in the excitement of seeing Sharkey's thoughts on the computer screen. How could she have forgotten the very reason she'd persuaded Marvin to use Mom's computer? "He has to get your collar off," she told Sharkey.

It wasn't so hot this morning, Alison thought, as a breeze flowed through the screen door into the kitchen. Dad had already left, she realized with a glance at the clock on the stove. Too bad—she should have gotten a ride to Marvin's from him. It was always hard to pry her mother away from her desk in the basement.

But today Alison was in luck. Her mother had planned to go into Boston to the main library this morning, she said, and she didn't mind dropping Alison off on the way. "But Alison," her mother added, swinging around in her desk chair to give Alison a fierce look, "what is this phrase that keeps cropping up in my thesis this morning?" She jabbed her forefinger at a sheet of paper curling from the printer.

Oh, no, thought Alison. That kind of question it was better not to answer.

"MOUSE-DUNG," her mother answered herself.

Alison smiled weakly and backed out of the office. Upstairs, she fed Sharkey, ate some raisin bran, and popped the cat into his carrier with his catnip mouse. Then she was sorry she'd packed him before the last minute, because he began to meow.

The phone rang and Alison picked it up, expecting Marvin.

But it was Denise. "Hi! Guess what?" Denise sounded as excited as Alison had been about getting her kitten. "I think Sonia's going to join the club!" When Alison didn't say anything, she added, "Sonia said a beauty pageant would be hyper-mature. So we're going to have a club meeting this morning to plan the pageant. Ten o'clock, at my house. See you!"

"Wait!" exclaimed Alison, before Denise could hang up. "I can't come this morning. I have to go to Marvin's."

"Marvin Smith?" Denise sounded puzzled. "Why're you going to his house?"

Of course Denise wondered why Alison would be

spending the morning with an eighth-grade boy, and a peculiar one at that. But Alison wasn't sure she should tell Denise the truth.

Denise went on, "Can't you see him later? This is an important meeting. And it's the only time Sonia and Karen and Karen's cousin from Maine can all come."

Alison was afraid she ought to go to that meeting, just to protect her rights—although she didn't want to meet with Sonia, this morning or anytime. And why should she have to? How had this happened?

In only a day or so, Alison had gone from being the other half of the club to being just a member, a member Denise hadn't even consulted when she planned the meeting. If Denise had asked, of course Alison would have told her she couldn't come to a meeting this morning.

"I've *got* to go to Marvin's now. This is the only time my mom can give me a ride." Alison was feeling more and more edgy, between arguing with Denise and listening to Sharkey's meows.

"Why do you *have* to go to Marvin's?" Denise asked again. A sympathetic note crept into her voice. "You sound like something's the matter. What's the matter?"

A lot was the matter, and Alison needed a friend to talk to. In spite of a warning feeling, Alison couldn't help saying, "Okay, if you really want to know. Marvin's going to help me find out why Sharkey and all the rest of the cats around here have these weird collars. You know that story I read about the IRS using cats to spy on people? *It might be true.*"

There was a silence on the other end of the line.

Then Denise sighed one of her long sighs. "I wasn't going to tell you this, but maybe I should."

"What?" Alison felt a horrible tingle in her bones, the kind you feel looking off a cliff and thinking about falling all the way down. "Tell me what?"

"Well, all right, I'll tell you. But don't get mad." Another pause. "One reason Sonia wasn't sure she wanted to join the club was she thinks you pretend too much."

Alison felt breathless, as if she really were falling through space. "Pretend? *I* pretend too much?" Anger began to heat up her face, and she thought of how many things Denise had made believe about. Like her complicated plans for when the two of them got married, down to the two sets of brides and grooms on the wedding cake and the argument about who got to walk down the aisle first. "And *you* don't pretend? You're the one who always wanted to pretend about the double wedding."

"Yeah, but that's different, don't you understand?" Denise spoke in her patient, kindly tone. "I mean, you pretend things that couldn't really happen. Like when you thought you were winning chess games because of Marvin Smith's invention."

"But I was," said Alison slowly. Wearing Marvin's machine had made her stop being nervous, so she could concentrate on the game. She'd told Denise that.

Then, as if she'd finally hit the ground, Alison felt the shock of what Denise had done. "You told *her?* You told Sonia my secret that I told you not to tell anyone?"

"I was afraid you'd get mad," said Denise sorrow-fully. "It's not as if I told a secret about something real. How could a machine Marvin made out of a Walkman help you win chess games?"

"I . . . was . . . *not* . . . pretending!" But Alison knew Denise wouldn't believe her. She could imagine, all too well, Denise and Sonia discussing the problem of Alison and her pretend games. In her mind's eye their heads were bent close as they talked, Denise's pale stringy hair almost touching Sonia's cloud of moussed and scrunched-up brown hair. She felt sick.

Denise started to say something else, but now Alison saw her mother opening the basement door. "All set?" asked Mrs. Harrity.

"I have to go," Alison said curtly. She hoped her tone of voice told Denise how much she wanted to smack her. "Bye."

At the Smiths' house, in a new development on the other side of Rushfield, Marvin's mother opened the door for Alison. It was uncanny, Alison thought, how much Mrs. Smith looked like her son, except that she was a woman, and tall.

"It's so nice of you to let Marvin use your cat for his experiment, dear." She waved Alison up the stairs. "Tell him the girls and I have a couple of errands to do, and then I'll come up and take some pictures."

Pictures? wondered Alison. But Mrs. Smith was herding Marvin's little sisters out the door.

Although the summer day was bright and clear, once Alison stepped into Marvin's room with its closed drapes, she might have been underground on another planet. She'd been to Marvin's once before, last spring, to ask for help with the chess tournament. But she'd forgotten how weird this room looked, with the star maps on the ceiling, the mobile of the solar system bobbing over the bed, and the large poster of a human brain on one wall.

The computer was already humming, and Marvin was hunched over the keyboard. But he jumped up as Alison came in. "Okay! Let's hook up the subject and go for it."

There was something Alison didn't like about his tone. "Did you figure out a way to get the collars off?" she asked as she let Sharkey out of his carrier. The cat bounded onto the top of the computer, as if that were his reserved seat.

"Get the collars off?" Frowning, Marvin taped the electrodes onto Sharkey's collar. "Then we'd never intercept any messages." Before Alison could protest, he added quickly, "Of course I *will* find out how to get them off. It'll be a natural by-product of solving this mystery." He bent over the keyboard. Sharkey stretched out on top of the computer with his striped tail hanging over the screen.

"So what are you doing now?" asked Alison. Marvin didn't answer; he just frowned and waved at the tail. Alison rearranged the cat so that his tail hung over the side of the computer.

While Alison petted Sharkey, Marvin tapped the keyboard and muttered to himself. "Something weird about this. Receptors for incoming code don't fit any of these patterns." He got up to adjust the connector at the back of the computer and the electrodes attached to Sharkey's collar. He tapped and muttered some more, and then he picked up a booklet titled *CodeCracker* and studied it. "That should do it, if—" He went back to tapping and muttering.

Alison knew Marvin expected her to shut up and wait, but finally she couldn't stand it any longer. She would give Marvin a choice: Either he told her what was going on, or she'd take Sharkey and go home.

But just at that moment, Marvin made a sound of disgust. "Ech!" He slumped back in his chair, glaring at the screen.

"What's the matter?" asked Alison.

For a moment Marvin didn't answer. Then he glanced up at Alison as if he was surprised to see her still standing there. "There's nothing to decode," he said shortly.

"But . . . You mean the collar isn't for sending messages after all?"

"No. That's what it's for, all right. But it doesn't send them all the time." Marvin looked at her with his head to one side. "How many times did you see Sharkey acting weird? I mean, twitching and all that?"

"Once."

"And how many times did you see the Thompsons' cat acting weird?"

"Once." Alison was beginning to see what he meant.

"Yeah. And I saw this cat down the street having one of those 'fits'—once. If the cats have their 'fits' when they get messages, then they don't get them very often. So we could be here all day and not get any further than this." Marvin gestured angrily at the screen.

Lifting her hands from Sharkey, who was now asleep, Alison stepped to Marvin's side and bent to read the screen. The heading at the top said, MESSAGE. Halfway down another heading said, REPLY. At the right-hand upper corner the screen displayed, ENTER CODED MESSAGE. "I see," said Alison. "You can't enter any message until they send one."

"If it came, *I* wouldn't actually enter it," said Marvin. "It would enter automatically, through that." He pointed to the wire that ran from Sharkey's collar to the back of the computer.

Alison looked thoughtfully at the wire, then back at Marvin. "Too bad about the messages," she said. "Well, why don't you work on finding the fastener thing in the collar? I bet—"

Rowrl, said Sharkey in a complaining tone. Turning back to him, Alison drew her breath in sharply. The pupils of the cat's yellow eyes were widening, and his ears slowly flattened.

"They're sending," whispered Marvin. "Code-Cracker, do your stuff."

Alison pressed her knuckles against her mouth. Poor Sharkey! The cat's tongue was sticking out a little, his ears and whiskers beginning to twitch. Lights were twinkling, dancing in a pattern, inside the clear substance of his collar.

Marvin's gaze flicked down to the computer screen. He gasped and pointed.

Under the heading MESSAGE, new letters marched across the screen: SKY GUYS TO WHITE CAT SKY GUYS TO WHITE CAT.

· *10* ·

Big Mama

"Yeah, baby!" whispered Marvin, sliding into his chair again. Alison stooped beside him, her heart pounding. Even though she'd been sure the collars were controlling the cats, it was shocking to see evidence right on Marvin's computer screen. SKY GUYS TO WHITE CAT, repeated the message.

Sharkey snarled, and an answer flashed under REPLY: GET OUT OF HERE GET THIS MOUSE-DUNG COLLAR OFF ME NOW NOW NOW I BITE YOUR TENTACLES OFF.

The computer gave a sharp beep. Sharkey jerked and meowed. ERROR REPLY, the message scolded.

Alison winced and put a hand on the cat. "Poor Sharkey!"

"Quiet." Marvin flapped a hand at her.

Sharkey's ears flattened even closer to his head. His new response appeared on the screen: HERE / READY.

Immediately another message commanded, RE-PORT LIFE-FORMS PRESENT.

Sharkey gazed at Alison, and letters formed on the screen: BIG MAMA.

"Hee!" Marvin sputtered with sudden laughter. "That's what he calls you."

Then the cat turned his yellow eyes on Marvin. MONKEY BOY.

It was Alison's turn to giggle, glancing at Marvin. He didn't laugh this time.

On the computer screen, a new order appeared: REPORT RESOURCES IN AREA.

Sharkey surveyed the room, sniffing the air, as he began to respond with a list:

BED (FOR NAPS)
WIGGLY BALLS ON WIRES (PLAY)

There was another sharp beep, and again Sharkey jerked and meowed. INAPPROPRIATE DATA, the screen scolded. REPORT URANIUM ORE REPORT FOSSIL FUELS REPORT HYDRO- ELECTRIC POTENTIAL.

"It's not fair!" exclaimed Alison. "He doesn't know about any of those things."

Marvin started to say something, but just then there was a knock on the door of his room. Mrs. Smith, a camera in one hand, stepped in. "Photo opportunity time!" She held the camera up to her face. "Marvin, look as if you're making a discovery. Oh, Grandma Louise will love this one. Alison, stay in the picture—you can be Marvin's little assistant. Perfect!" The flash went off.

Sharkey crouched down on the computer top, making himself as flat as he could. He let out a low wail. MOUSE-DUNG was his reply to the last message.

"Is the kitty all right?" Mrs. Smith, poised to take

another picture, lowered her camera. "Marvin, I hope you aren't doing anything to hurt Alison's cat."

"I'm *not*," growled Marvin. "And I'm on the edge of the breakthrough of—" He stopped and leaned forward to read a new message on the screen. So did Alison, but it seemed the "Sky Guys" had decided there was nothing more to get out of Sharkey right now: DATA RECORDED   END OF REPORT. The computer sighed loudly as Marvin shut it down.

Even before Marvin removed the electrodes from Sharkey's collar, the cat burst into a loud, frightened purr and crawled into Alison's arms. He pushed his head into the sleeve of her knit shirt as if he wanted to climb inside.

"Marvin," said Mrs. Smith sternly. "I know this is science and all, but I don't think you're treating the cat very well. I'm going to take Alison and her pet home right now."

"Whatever you say," muttered Marvin. He added, just loud enough for Alison but not his mother to hear, "Monkey Mama."

That was exactly what Sharkey *would* call Mrs. Smith, thought Alison. Snorting from trying not to laugh, she lifted Sharkey back into his carrier and followed Marvin's mother down the stairs.

On the way home Alison thought of explaining to Mrs. Smith that it was the collar itself, not Marvin's wiring, punishing Sharkey. But she realized before she opened her mouth that she'd have to tell about the *Weekly Informer* and the IRS, and Mrs. Smith would never believe her.

"At least I got a nice picture," remarked Mrs. Smith

as Alison climbed out of the car at the end of her driveway. "Grandma Louise doesn't need to know the unpleasant part."

Alison walked slowly up the gravel driveway, lugging Sharkey in his carrier. The unpleasant part, in her opinion, was that Sharkey's collar was still on, in spite of Marvin's talk about a "by-product." In fact, she thought with a sinking feeling, Marvin must want to keep Sharkey's collar *on* until he learned as much as possible about whoever was sending the messages. How long was that going to take?

At the top of the steps from the driveway to the side door, Alison was surprised to see a pink envelope rolled and stuck in the handle of the screen door. She set the cat carrier down and pulled the envelope out.

It was a note from Denise, written on Denise's special pink paper decorated with a picture of a kitten sniffing a flower. *Minutes of the Last Meeting* said the heading in Denise's small, careful printing.

Oh, yes—the meeting of the Candy Club that Alison had missed this morning. But it looked like it wasn't the Candy Club anymore.

All the members present at the meeting, except for one member who could have been there but wasn't, the note continued, *decided to change the name of the club from the Candy Club to the P&P Club, because that is more mature. P&P means Poised 'n' Pretty.*

More like Pushy 'n' Pains, thought Alison.

The members of the P&P Club, the memo
went on, *decided to have more mature
activities. Our next activity will be the Miss
Preteen Rushfield beauty pageant. It will take
place tomorrow afternoon at 3:00 at 34
Chestnut Hill Road.*

That was Alison's house. Denise had a nerve, not
even checking with Alison about whether it was all
right to have the pageant at her house. Of course Mrs.
Farino, Denise's mother, would never let them put on
a pageant at *her* spick-and-span house. She might even
think the whole idea was "unsavory."

Refolding the pink note paper, Alison wondered
what Denise would think if Alison told her about her
morning at Marvin's. Would Denise believe that Alison
had seen strange messages from somebody or other to
Sharkey on Marvin's computer? Or was she so
wrapped up in being mature and impressing Sonia
that she'd just insist Alison was pretending again?

In the kitchen Alison let Sharkey out of his carrier.
It made her feel bad, the way he purred and rubbed
against her leg. Big Mama, he called her. He probably
thought she could take care of him and protect him,
but she couldn't even get that cruel collar off his neck.
"I'm not as great as you think," she told Sharkey,
stroking his back. But he only gazed up at her with
half-closed eyes and kept on purring.

Wondering what to do next, Alison found a bunch of
grapes in the refrigerator and took it out on the deck.
Sharkey chased a stray grape across the boards, pounc-

ing on it and biting it until it was too squished to roll.

That's what he'd like to do to whoever put the collar on him, thought Alison. I wish he could, too.

Her mind swung back to the messages she'd seen on Marvin's computer screen. It struck her, now, how strange they were. They wanted Sharkey to report on "resources," like uranium ore. But they must know he was a cat, because they'd put his collar on him. So why—

Suddenly a hand reached over Alison's shoulder and pulled a grape from the bunch. "Hey!" said Alison, whirling around.

She was surprised at how serious and steady Maureen's gaze was as she sat down in the next chair and munched the grape. Alison was about to tell her sister to get her own grapes when Maureen spoke up. "What's Marvin trying to get you into?"

"Nothing," said Alison. "He was just trying to help me get Sharkey's collar off." That wasn't true, of course. It was what she wanted Marvin to do, all right, but so far he hadn't even tried.

Maureen gave her a disbelieving look. "I bet he's setting you up for something. You don't really believe that *Weekly Informer* story about the IRS putting collars on cats, do you?"

"I don't think it was the IRS," admitted Alison. "Because the messages—"

"Not the IRS?" asked Maureen with a mocking smile. "Then it must have been an alien. Yeah! The same one that *munched* the *mailman!*"

Alison drew her breath in sharply. *Yes*. Because human beings, no matter how stupid they were or what part of the world they came from, would never think a cat could tell them anything about uranium ore.

"Look," Maureen went on. "I know Marvin. He's probably doing an experiment about how people react when they think aliens are coming, or something like that. He could pull it off—you should have seen the special effects he did for the eighth-grade play."

Alison was hardly listening. And hadn't Sharkey mentioned TENTACLES? *Aliens . . .*

"Alison!" Maureen was leaning forward, snapping her fingers in front of Alison's face. "Don't you remember what happened last spring, when you let Marvin try out that invention on you?"

Somehow the fact that Alison had thought of that herself only made her angry at Maureen. "It's not exactly any of your business, Maureen."

Her sister shrugged and stood up. "Don't say I didn't warn you. Well, I can't watch you every minute—I'm going over to Tara's."

Alison scowled at Maureen's back as her sister padded barefoot into the house. But then she shivered. Aliens, little gray people with huge eyes like insects, as the *Weekly Informer* often pictured them?

Sharkey rubbed against her ankle, and she stroked him absently. They had him in their power—as long as he was wearing the collar.

Maybe Maureen was right, in a way. Alison should try to get help from someone besides Marvin. It was too bad Mom wasn't home. Alison wouldn't try to convince her mother about the messages on Marvin's computer screen, of course. But if Alison insisted that

Sharkey's collar was bothering him, Mom would try to think of a way to get it off.

But Mom wasn't here. And the person who really ought to help Alison was Denise. A surge of anger pushed Alison to her feet. Yes, Denise owed Alison something, if she expected Alison to have the beauty pageant at her house. Denise should understand that she had to listen to Alison and help her.

With Sharkey following, Alison went back inside to the kitchen phone. She was still confident as she dialed Denise's number, but at the first ring she realized Denise wasn't going to see it her way.

In fact, Denise wasn't even home. Mrs. Farino's polite voice said, "She went to Sonia's house, and I *think* she'll be there all afternoon. Can I have her call you this evening?"

Alison was so taken aback that she couldn't answer. Denise had already spent part of the morning with Sonia. Now she was spending all afternoon with her, too? Until a couple of days ago, Alison had been the one Denise spent that much time with.

"Or maybe you'd like to call again later," suggested Mrs. Farino.

"Uh . . . okay. I mean, it isn't important."

Isn't important? Hanging up the phone, Alison thought that there was nothing more important than getting help. But it looked like she couldn't count on Denise for any.

· 11 ·

Sharkey in Danger

It was almost dinnertime when Mrs. Harrity got home from Boston. She waved to Alison, who was on the family-room floor trying to play chess while Sharkey batted the pieces, and then went straight to the phone.

Alison didn't pay much attention until she heard her mother say, "Yes, that's why I called—I know there are some serious diseases that cats can give to humans." Then her mother described Sharkey's "fit." "His tongue was sticking out, and his ears and whiskers were twitching."

Alison felt a sudden icy lump in her stomach. She picked Sharkey off the chessboard and held him against her shoulder while she stroked him. He nibbled at a button on her shirt collar.

After a silence, Mrs. Harrity spoke into the phone again. "We'll watch him closely, then." She hung up and turned to Alison with a sober face. "Darling, I don't want to worry you, but if Sharkey—well, if he has any more fits, we'll have to take him to . . . to the vet's."

"There's nothing wrong with him!" Alison stood up, holding her cat tighter. "And he's my cat, not yours to do whatever you want with."

"This isn't a matter of what I want," said Mrs. Harrity heavily. "It's a matter of the family's health. The vet said that twitching and so on might be the first signs of a rare neurological disease—a disease of the nerves."

"Mom! I can't believe you're talking this way. Sharkey doesn't have any disease. It's just that his collar—"

"We don't know whether he has this disease," said her mother in a frighteningly quiet voice. "If he does, the vet says the kindest thing would be to—"

"You just want to get rid of Sharkey!" shouted Alison. Without meaning to, she squeezed Sharkey so hard that he squeaked. He struggled out of her arms and jumped down. "You didn't want a cat, and now you won't even let me have my cat." Alison didn't intend to start crying, but suddenly tears were running down her cheeks. "You're so mean, I can't believe it."

"Go to your room, Alison." Mrs. Harrity looked more at a loss than angry. "You're not being reasonable."

Alison was already heading in the direction of her room, following Sharkey down the hall. "If Sharkey goes, I go," she flung over her shoulder.

Alison wasn't in her room for long before her father called her to set the table. But by then Alison had decided she would try to be calm. Maybe her mother had thought things over, too; maybe Mom was sorry she'd jumped to the conclusion that Sharkey had a disease.

Dinner was tuna salad and French bread, which ordinarily Alison liked a lot. But tonight her mother made her leave Sharkey inside while they ate on the deck. Alison knew, without her mother explaining, that it was because she thought he had germs.

Sharkey meowed the whole time. He stood on his hind legs with his white belly stretched out full-length and his front paws up on the glass of the sliding door. Alison knew what he was trying to tell her, as if his thoughts were flashing on a screen in her mind: OUT, BIG MAMA? PLEASE OUT, BIG MAMA? PLEASE?

"You're not eating anything, Alison," said her father. "Never mind Sharkey. He'll be happy enough when he gets the tuna scraps."

"Oh, no," said Mrs. Harrity. "Frank, I told you what the vet said. We can't let Sharkey lick our plates. What if . . ." She looked at Alison and stopped.

"Anyway, he's calming down," said her father.

Alison turned back toward Sharkey, and her heart sank. He'd pulled his paws down from the door and was sitting there, staring into space. She was afraid she could see a bit of pink tongue sticking out of his mouth. And wasn't his collar beginning to sparkle? "I'm getting more milk," she almost shouted, swinging her legs over the picnic bench.

As she shoved the sliding door open, her father remarked with a puzzled laugh, "Such an urgent desire for milk."

Alison swept the cat up and hustled him away down

85

the hall to her room. Whatever they thought, Mom and Dad mustn't see Sharkey having another "fit."

Closing and locking her door, Alison sat on her bed holding Sharkey. The "fit" of twitching ears and whiskers was over, but now Sharkey growled. Then he gave a little jerk, and his ears flattened.

"Poor Sharkey," said Alison. Still, a smile twitched her lips as she thought of the message he must be sending: MOUSE−DUNG COLLAR. That collar! How was she going to get it off? Alison still thought Marvin could do it if he wanted to. But the one who really ought to help, if she was any kind of a friend, was Denise.

A picture came to Alison's mind, as it had this morning, of Denise with Sonia. Her stomach clenched. She put Sharkey down on the bed, where he began to wash himself, and got out her diary.

First she wrote down how Denise had been acting about Sonia. Then she wrote, *I don't know if I have a best friend anymore.*

That looked even worse on paper than it had felt in her mind, so Alison went quickly on to the next thing:

Someone's sending messages to Sharkey with the collar. I think they're aliens. Marvin is supposed to find out how to get the collar off, but I don't think he cares. I'm scared.

That didn't make her feel any better, either. Alison swallowed hard. And there was something even worse, which she didn't have the heart to tell her diary: about Mom and the vet.

Alison locked the diary, as if she could lock up the disturbing thoughts she'd been thinking, and started to push it under her mattress as usual. Then she hesitated. She'd been sort of playing a game with Maureen about hiding her diary, almost intending her sister to find it when she snooped. But the thoughts Alison had just written were private. None of Maureen's business.

"Where should I hide it?" she asked Sharkey, stroking him. "A really good hiding place."

The cat arched his back and rubbed against Alison's arm. Then he crouched and pounced across the bed, seizing Curious George by the neck.

Alison giggled at the wild expression in Sharkey's eyes. "Don't bite the poor monkey—he didn't put your collar on." She pried the stuffed toy from Sharkey's paws.

"Hey, Sharkey, you're a genius!" The cat had made a rip in the back of Curious George's head, a rip just large enough to tuck in a diary key. It wouldn't matter if Maureen found the diary, as long as she couldn't find the key.

Just as Alison finished hiding the diary and the key, there was a knock on her door. Probably Mom, wanting her to come back and finish dinner. Alison took her time about answering.

But it was Marvin. His brown eyes, serious and excited, shone in a way that almost frightened her. "I thought I should tell you this in person," he said. "You know that article about the IRS using cats to spy on people? What a bunch of fools. Guess who really put Sharkey's collar on—who put all the cats' collars on?"

"Aliens," said Alison.

Marvin's mouth dropped open. The weird shine left his eyes. "How did you know? Well—never mind. Bring the cat down to the computer. I've got to do some more work with the collar." He tipped his shirt pocket open with one finger, showing a computer disk and coil of wire.

"Just a minute," said Alison as Marvin hurried back down the hall. "Mom got mad when she found cat swearwords in her thesis this morning. She doesn't like to let anyone else use her computer."

"She doesn't have to know, does she? It won't take that long. They'll be out on the deck for a while, right?"

Alison shrugged and nodded. So what if Mom did get mad? After all, *Alison* was mad at *Mom*, talking about putting Sharkey away for a disease he didn't even have. "Mom and Dad usually sit out there and talk until the mosquitoes get bad." Then she remembered what she had wanted to say to Marvin. "But I'm not going to go along with this unless you get Sharkey's collar off!" she burst out.

"Shh." Marvin looked over his shoulder. "Sure, of course. But *they're* the only ones who can do it. That's why I have to make contact with them first."

Alison wasn't exactly satisfied with this, but she could see she didn't have much choice. She picked up Sharkey and led Marvin down the basement stairs. They both tiptoed, not saying anything until they were in Mrs. Harrity's office. With swift movements Marvin switched the computer on and booted up his program, adding electronic beeps and gurgles to the hum of the dehumidifier. As he was taping the electrodes onto Sharkey's collar, he remarked, "You know, I've been thinking about something. I wonder if I made the wrong assumption."

"What do you mean?" asked Alison, rubbing Sharkey under his fuzzy white chin. "You think they *aren't* aliens after all?"

"No. No, they're aliens all right. I mean, I just went along with the assumption they made in that stupid article—that someone was using the collars to spy on people."

"But they are, aren't they?" Alison frowned. "They asked Sharkey about us."

"No." Marvin shook his head. "They just asked about life-forms—that means any kind of plants or animals. I don't think the aliens even know what human beings are. If they're only talking to cats, they might get completely the wrong impression."

Like that you're a MONKEY BOY. Alison smiled to herself. Then thinking about the messages reminded her of something. "You might not get any messages now. Sharkey just had a 'fit' a little while ago."

"No problem," said Marvin, scooting Mrs. Harrity's chair up to the computer. "I can find out a lot just by analyzing the structure of the collars."

"What do you mean?" Alison set Sharkey down on top of the computer and watched the screen over Marvin's shoulder. But she couldn't make any sense out of the diagrams and rows of symbols she saw.

Marvin frowned a little, as if he would rather concentrate on the computer than answer her questions.

"Like for instance, I can see here that the collar has a pretty short range. Whoever's sending the messages is within thirty thousand miles of the Earth." He glanced up at Alison, who still didn't quite understand. "That means they aren't sitting out on Pluto or someplace. They're in orbit around the Earth."

"Right up there?" Alison glanced up at the white squares of the office ceiling. She felt a chill, from more than the cool air of the basement. As though a dot high in the sky had cast a shadow on her.

If Marvin had any creepy feelings about the aliens above them, he didn't show it. Hitching the chair closer to the computer, he bent over the keyboard.

While Alison fidgeted and petted Sharkey, Marvin tapped and muttered and the computer beeped and clicked. "Yeah, baby!" he exclaimed at one point. Finally he sat up and stretched. "I don't want to make you nervous, but I think you should know about this."

"Know what?" asked Alison nervously. She backed up to stare at the screen. The diagrams and symbols looked different now, but not any easier to understand.

"Okay." Marvin gave a little laugh. "I can hardly believe this myself, but all the data seem to point to the same thing. *These collars aren't just for sending messages.*"

"What do you mean?" Alison was baffled. "What else are they for, then?"

Marvin paused a moment before he spoke. "Transportation."

· *12* ·

Don't Panic

"Transportation?" Alison had an image of little carts hooked up to the cats' collars. "Transport what—resources?"

"Uh-uh," said Marvin. "Themselves." He added, "You know how they do it on 'Star Trek,' beaming themselves down from the ship to the planet they're exploring?"

" 'Star Trek'?" repeated Alison. The more Marvin talked, the more she wondered if Maureen was right. Maybe Marvin *had* latched onto a science-fiction idea and gotten carried away with it. "You mean there's a beaming thing in the cats' collars?" She touched the clear ring around Sharkey's neck. "How could it be that little?"

"No, not the whole system." Marvin seemed amused that she could ask such a thing. "Just one part of it. Like . . . Let's see, I'm trying to think of something simple to compare it to. Like the pulley on one end of a ski lift, you know? It's not the part that actually carries you, but you have it to make the thing work."

Alison thought about this for a moment. "So—you mean any place there's a cat with a collar on, they could appear there?" She looked around her mother's little office, which had barely enough room for her and Marvin and Sharkey. "Like here?"

"Yeah, but listen," said Marvin hastily. "If it happens, *don't panic.* There's no reason to think they're hostile. Whatever you do, don't do anything to alarm them."

'Alison was alarmed herself at the way Marvin's eyes were glittering. She suddenly remembered a scary movie, one she wished she hadn't watched. Those aliens had been like giant insects that fed humans to their larvae.

"I'll need to borrow Sharkey for a while, to work at home," Marvin went on. He turned off the computer, unhooked the cat, and gathered his equipment. "Let's find some rope, and I'll strap his carrier on the back of my bike. Or maybe your dad could give me a ride home."

"*No,* you can't borrow Sharkey." Alison didn't want to get Marvin mad at her, but she didn't trust him that much. "Maybe I could bring him over again tomorrow, though."

Marvin frowned, then shrugged. "Never mind. I'll work with one of the cats in my neighborhood."

But at the top of the basement stairs, Marvin turned to Alison and added, "Do you understand how big this thing is? This is bigger than the first moon landing.

92

This is contact with an intelligent extraterrestrial species!" He had a faraway look, as if he were imagining
himself receiving a Nobel prize. "And I'm making the
contact."

The next morning, just after she'd fed Sharkey his
breakfast, the phone rang. Alison hoped it was Marvin,
with some helpful discovery.

But it was Denise. "I'm coming over to set up for
the Miss Preteen Rushfield pageant," she said. "We
have to get the props and everything ready before-
hand, because three o'clock is sort of late. But we
couldn't do the pageant any earlier, because Sonia had
to go to July sales with her mom."

"I don't know if this is such a good time," protested
Alison. With Denise here, it might be hard to watch
Sharkey closely enough. "I—I might have to do some-
thing important this morning."

"What are you talking about?" Denise sounded indignant. "This is the day of the pageant. Are you in
the club or not? Besides setting up, you have to get
your costumes together."

"Yes, but Denise . . ." Alison hesitated, then blurted
it out. "Something awful. My mom called the vet
about Sharkey, and the vet said he might have a bad
disease, and Mom's thinking about putting Sharkey to
sleep." Her voice cracked on the last word, and she
realized how much she'd missed talking to her best
friend about what was upsetting her.

"That's terrible!" Denise spoke in a shocked and
sympathetic tone, like the friend Alison wanted her to

be. "Why does your mom think he's sick? Is he throwing up?"

Alison hesitated. "No. . . . He twitches sometimes, and his tongue sticks out. But he isn't sick." She wanted so much to tell Denise the whole story, although something warned her not to. "Denise, listen. I found out—I found out that it's Sharkey's collar that gives him fits. He gets them when the aliens—"

She stopped. Careful. Explain it all so Denise will understand. "See, Marvin hooked up Sharkey's collar to his computer so we could listen in on the messages. And they have to be aliens, because they asked Sharkey about uranium ore—see, human beings wouldn't do that."

Alison paused again, feeling desperate. Denise wasn't saying anything. Alison must not be explaining it right. "I *saw* Sharkey have another fit, and it was when the aliens were sending him messages."

"I knew it," said Denise. For a hopeful moment Alison thought her friend meant that she believed her. But Denise went on, "This is just what Sonia says happens to people who pretend too much—they start believing what they're pretending."

"But I saw the messages. On Marvin's computer." Alison spoke in a low, desperate voice.

"Alison," said Denise sharply. "You have to promise me: Don't say *anything* about this to Sonia. She's still kind of iffy about the club, if you know what I mean."

Denise wouldn't even consider that Alison might be telling the exact truth. All Denise cared about was what Sonia thought. Denise was afraid that if she got talked into believing Alison, then Sonia would think she was pretending, too.

"So anyway," Denise went on as if that were all settled, "I'm coming over to set up."

A short while later Denise appeared at the side door. She was smiling as if she'd forgotten about Alison's embarrassing alien-messages talk. "Help me carry some things in, will you?"

Down on the driveway, the saddlebags of Denise's bike were full of boxes and shopping bags. "What's all that stuff?" asked Alison. "I thought you were just bringing over a few props."

Denise handed Alison two boxes. "I thought I might as well bring over my evening gown and bathing suit and high heels, too. So when I come over this afternoon, I'll just wear my outfit for the ensemble dance number and bring the lighting." She glanced at Alison as if she was sizing her up. "Did you get all your costumes together?"

"Er . . . not all of them." Alison didn't want to tell Denise that she'd hardly given the pageant a thought since she read Denise's minutes of the last meeting. "I guess I could wear my Middle Ages robe from the chess tournament for an evening gown."

"Your Middle Ages robe!" Denise looked shocked. "That's not anything like an evening gown. Your gown has to be strapless, or at least just have little straps. You can't have sleeves."

"That's ridiculous," exclaimed Alison. "Where am I going to get a strapless dress?"

"I guess I'm lucky," admitted Denise. "My cousin let me borrow her old prom dress. It'd be really mature if it had sequins, but at least it's only a little bit loose, because she's short. And she had matching high heels, and her feet are small, too. I already practiced walking in them."

"In her feet?" Alison giggled.

Denise only frowned, as if it were childish of Alison to joke about high heels. "Sonia has a great outfit that she found at the thrift shop," she went on. "And dance shoes with little heels."

"It's not my fault I don't have a cousin who went to the prom," snapped Alison. "Or that I didn't have time to go to the thrift shop."

"You know, I have an idea." From Denise's carefully casual tone, and the way she looked sideways at Alison from behind her glasses, Alison thought that Denise must have had the idea a while ago.

"Since you don't even have an evening gown yet," Denise went on brightly, "maybe you shouldn't try to be a contestant."

"Well, thanks a lot, Denise!" Alison balanced both boxes in one arm to open the screen door, trying not to trip as Sharkey wound himself around her ankles. "You're going to use my house, but you want me to just sit there and watch?"

"No, no," said Denise. "You're so touchy. What I mean is, there's something very important we forgot about. We need a host."

"Oh, you mean the guy who interviews the girls." Alison wasn't paying full attention to Denise, because she was trying to keep an eye on Sharkey. That wasn't easy, with the boxes blocking her view of her feet, and Sharkey trying to rub against her legs while she was walking.

"Right," said Denise eagerly. "And he introduces them, and talks about how lovely they are and where they're from and so on."

Alison led the way through the kitchen. "But what would I wear?" she asked over her shoulder. "I don't have a man's suit, and I couldn't wear my father's. And I'd feel stupid, trying to think of things to say." Especially about how lovely you are, she added silently.

"Don't worry." Looking pleased with herself, Denise nodded at one of the boxes in Alison's arms. "I brought my brother's suit for you. And I wrote out your script, so you don't have to think of anything to say."

Alison stalked into her room and dropped the boxes on the bed. Denise had a lot of nerve, planning all this without consulting her. Worse, Alison was sure that Denise *had* consulted Sonia. "Don't you think she's a little immature to be a contestant?" Alison could imagine Sonia asking Denise.

And Denise would agree with anything Sonia said, because the main purpose of the beauty pageant was to get Denise in good with Sonia.

· 13 ·

Mature Activities

"Hey!" exclaimed Denise. Sharkey had jumped onto the bed and was trying to push his nose under the lid of one of the boxes. "That's my evening gown."

"He isn't hurting anything." Alison pulled Sharkey away from the box and settled him on her shoulder. "Come on, let's go check out the living room."

In the living room Sharkey jumped from Alison's shoulder to the lid of the stereo. He stretched out one hind leg and spread his toes so that he could lick between them. Then he sat up, watching the girls with wide yellow eyes. Maybe, thought Alison hopefully, the aliens are fed up with him, and they won't send him any more messages.

"Yes, this is a good room," said Denise with satisfaction, putting one foot on the raised hearth. "See, this is like a little stage. The host can stand here to interview the contestants." She turned and seized a floor lamp from beside the armchair. "And this is just right for a microphone." She unplugged the lamp, removed the shade and light bulb, and set the lamp/microphone on the hearth.

"The trouble is," Denise went on, facing the fireplace, "we need some palm trees or something to make it look like Florida. You know how they always have beauty pageants in Florida."

"We could make a backdrop," suggested Alison, getting into the spirit. "We could paint palm trees on a sheet."

Denise shook her head. "We don't have time. Hey!" Behind her glasses, her eyes widened with excitement. "Doesn't the shower curtain in your bathroom have palm trees?"

It did, but after they'd unhooked the curtain from its rings and hung it over the fireplace with pushpins, Denise didn't look satisfied. "Those gray streaks are mildew," she said. "Your mother should wash the curtain."

"You'd better not talk to *her* like that," said Alison, "or she won't let us have the pageant here. She made me promise we'd be quiet, because her office is right downstairs."

"Oh, well." Denise surveyed the room again, her eyes sparkling. "This is going to be so mature!" She pointed to the sofa opposite the fireplace. "The judge can sit there."

"And *he* can be the audience." Alison waved her hand at Sharkey on top of the stereo. Jumping down, Sharkey sniffed at the bottom of the mildewed shower curtain and at the base of the lamp. Then he padded to the sliding door, meowing.

Alison let him out, thinking about something else.

"But hey, just a minute. You said the judge can sit on the sofa. What judge?"

"I thought maybe Maureen—"

"That's a terrible idea!" exclaimed Alison. "She'll just make fun of us. Why can't Karen be the judge?"

Denise looked stubborn. "I promised Sonia I'd get someone mature. Not someone who might just pick anybody. The judge is very important. The whole point of a beauty pageant is one girl wins, and then she's crowned queen and gets a lot of prizes. Sonia's going to think it's stupid if . . ."

Alison looked sideways at her friend. If Sonia isn't crowned queen, she finished the sentence. Because this whole pageant is supposed to be about how wonderful she is.

At that moment Maureen strode into the living room. "Hey, Maureen," began Denise delightedly.

But Alison could see that Maureen had something serious on her mind. Ignoring Denise, her older sister folded her arms and fixed Alison with a frown. "Alison, how gullible are you? After I warned you about Marvin's experiments!"

With a shock Alison realized what Maureen knew and how she must have found out. "You read my diary!" How had Maureen found the key, so cleverly hidden in Curious George?

"Never mind," said Maureen sternly. "Listen to me: Marvin isn't interested in helping you, because he set the whole thing up. And besides, if there really were aliens, and he saw them slicing you up for sandwiches, he'd just stand there taking notes to report to his Professor Youngman."

"I don't have any privacy whatsoever in this house!" exclaimed Alison. "Okay. This is it. I'm telling. And I hope Mom grounds you until—until you go to college!"

"Excuse me, Maureen." Denise smiled her most winning smile, making her round cheeks even rounder. "We're having a preteen beauty pageant. And since you know a lot about fashion and you're in the intermediate school and everything, we thought we'd invite you to be the judge."

"A beauty pageant?" For a moment Maureen stared at Denise as if she thought her sister's friend must be out of her mind. Then a little smile appeared on her face. "A beauty pageant? You're going to have the pageant right here, this afternoon?" She shrugged. "Sure, why not? If I don't have anything better to do."

"Thanks!" Denise beamed at her. "I made scorecards for you. All you have to do is hold them up."

As Maureen left the room with a careless wave of her hand, Alison turned on Denise. "What did you do that for? The only reason Maureen wants to judge the pageant is so she can keep an eye on me. That, and so she can laugh at us."

Denise gazed back at Alison with a puzzled smile. "I didn't know you liked Marvin." She cleared her throat tactfully. "He isn't popular in the eighth grade, you know."

Alison stared at her friend in disgust. "Me? Like Marvin Smith?" Denise was so wrapped up in being a preteen that she'd lost touch with reality.

"What I can't figure out," Denise went on, "is why *Maureen* would like him. But obviously she's jealous of you going over to Marvin's."

102

Alison gave up, letting out a quiet groan. "Never mind. I'm thirsty. Let's get some juice."

In the kitchen, as Alison twisted the cap off a new bottle of cran-apple juice, she heard a meow by the side door. It must be Sharkey, but it wasn't his usual eager *R-row?* No, this meow had an angry sound. *Wowrlowrl.*

"It's Sharkey," said Denise, peering out the screened top of the door. "And look, it's that fluffy black cat from the neighbors' where you got him."

Looking over Denise's shoulder, Alison spotted Black Beauty crouching in the flower bed along the driveway. Sharkey was sitting on the back doorstep, glaring at the other cat and hissing. GET OUTTA HERE, Alison almost heard him say. Alison opened the door to let him in, but he stayed where he was without looking at her.

Black Beauty, a fluffy dark mop among the geraniums, blinked and looked away. But she didn't move, either. "What's she doing all the way over here?" Alison wondered. "The Thompsons hardly even let her out in their yard."

Then an answer came to her, and her stomach flipped. Black Beauty could be here because of a command she was getting from the alien collar around her neck. Did Marvin know anything about this?

"Weird," agreed Denise, turning back to the kitchen. "Well, how about that juice?"

Alison poured cran-apple juice for herself and Denise, but her mind was so full of what the cats were doing, and what it meant, that she had almost forgotten she was thirsty.

As soon as Denise had finished her juice, Alison went to the door and held it open pointedly. "I guess you have to get home for lunch," she told Denise. She could hardly wait for her friend to leave so she could call Marvin.

"Yeah—I'll go and come back this afternoon then," said Denise on her way out. "Of course I *could* invite myself for lunch," she added jokingly.

"Maybe you should invite yourself to Sonia's for lunch." Alison was a little shocked at her own tone of voice, but not really sorry.

Denise looked uneasy. "You aren't mad because I went to Sonia's yesterday afternoon, are you? It's just that we had to work on the dance routines for the pageant." When Alison didn't answer, she went on, "I didn't know you wanted to do anything yesterday. I thought you were at Marvin's."

Hm. Denise sounded worried that she might have pushed Alison too far about Sonia and the pageant. Well, she would just have to worry. Alison shut the screen door behind her friend with a firm click.

As soon as she saw Denise pedaling her bike out the driveway, Alison dialed Marvin's number. But it was the Smiths' answering machine, with Mrs. Smith's bright voice, that she got. "None of us are able to come to the phone right now," said the recording. "But if you'll leave your name and number, we'll get back to you as soon as we can."

Alison was too worried to think of a message for Marvin that would be safe for Mrs. Smith to hear. She'd have to call back.

• • •

After lunch Alison tried Marvin's number again, and got the recording again. This time she had a message prepared. "Marvin. I have some important scientific information for you. This is Alison."

Then Alison played a few chess games to calm herself, and tried to call Marvin again. Still the recording. She looked out the screen door to make sure Sharkey was there. Yes—he was sitting under a clump of day lilies, glaring at Black Beauty in the geraniums. Cats didn't seem to get bored as easily as humans.

Finally, in the middle of the afternoon, Marvin called her back. "I've got a major breakthrough going on here!" he announced. "Now, I want you to listen very carefully."

"A major breakthrough?" Alison almost shouted at him in her joy. Maureen had been completely wrong about Marvin. "You mean you found out how to get the collars off?"

"The collars! Give the collars a rest, will you? Just as I'm on the point of . . . Listen, here's what's going on." Marvin spoke slowly and distinctly. "I've established communication. I set them straight about cats and humans—I mean, that we're the dominant species here. And I found out they're from Aldebaran."

"You should listen to me," snapped Alison. "The Thompsons' cat is hanging around Sharkey, but I can tell it doesn't want to. Like someone's forcing them together."

"Both cats are at your house? Good. There's two Aldebarans, see—that's why they need the two cats with collars to beam down together from the orbiting spacecraft." Marvin sounded pleased. "I had some trouble communicating about the time I'd meet them, but I guess they got the general idea. Well, I've got some planning to do. Let me know as soon as they show up."

"Wait a minute!" exclaimed Alison. "The aliens can't come here this afternoon. We're having a beauty pageant. And what about—"

The line buzzed emptily—Marvin had hung up. Alison called right back, but now the answering machine, with Mrs. Smith's annoying, cheery voice, was on again.

A wave of fury rushed over Alison. "Marvin Smith," she said after the beep. "If you can communicate so well, you'd better communicate to get the collar off my friend. You know what I mean. Or I'll mess things up for *you.*"

Alison didn't know exactly what she'd do to mess things up, but she wanted Marvin to worry. What a nerve he had, arranging to meet the aliens at *her* house. She supposed he didn't want to get his mother upset, just as Denise didn't want to get her mother upset by holding the pageant at her house.

Alison stared at the kitchen clock. Two forty-five. The pageant was at three. And it would take her more than fifteen minutes to ride over to Marvin's and beat on him until he listened to her.

As Alison hesitated, she heard steps at the side door. "Almost pageant time!" called Denise. "Open the door, will you? My hands are full."

·14·

Poised 'n' Pretty

"What're you staring at, Alison?" Denise, wearing a leotard and shorts, jiggled the door handle with her elbow. "Open up—my hands are full. What are you looking at?"

"Nothing," said Alison truthfully, opening the door. She was peering over Denise's shoulder to see if the two cats were still in the flower bed, but they weren't. Maybe that was good—maybe the aliens were instructing the cats to go to Marvin's so they could beam down there.

But Alison didn't want that, either. She didn't want to let Sharkey out of her sight.

Denise stepped into the kitchen carrying a goose-neck desk lamp and a three-ring binder. "Here's your script," she told Alison, lifting several pages of lined paper from the binder. "Maybe you should start memorizing it. Of course, if we were really on television," she added with regret, "you could read from the TelePrompTer, and no one would know."

107

"No one will know anyway," said Alison, although she understood what Denise meant. If you were going to pretend that you were in a beauty pageant on television, you'd want everything as realistic as possible. Except that if Denise were realistic about herself, she would give up the whole idea.

Following Denise into the living room, Alison sat on the arm of a chair and wondered how she could explain Marvin's plans to Denise. A movement on the deck outside the sliding door caught her eye, and she drew her breath in sharply. Sharkey was there, meowing and snapping at his collar. Black Beauty crept after him, keeping her distance. The aliens were pushing the cats into position.

"A white spotlight at first," Denise was muttering to herself as she plugged in the lamp. "Then the pink spotlight, a change of mood, for the interview." She set a pink bulb on the end table. "Just before they announce the winner and the first runner-up. And crown Sonia . . . crown the winner Miss Preteen Rushfield." She placed a cardboard crown, which Alison recognized as Denise's White Queen crown from last spring's chess tournament, on the mantel.

"Denise," said Alison unhappily. "We can't have the pageant this afternoon."

Denise turned with a frown. "What do you mean? Everything's all set." She reached into one of her shopping bags for a bunch of fake flowers, which she put beside the crown. "Then they'll present her with the bouquet."

What could Alison say to convince Denise? She wouldn't listen to anything about aliens. "I—I just have a terrible feeling about this. Like a psychic feeling," she added hopefully. Denise liked stories in the *Weekly Informer* about people reading minds and predicting the future and so on.

Putting her hands on her hips, Denise looked at Alison the way you look at a little kid you have to humor. "This is about Sonia, isn't it? I wish you wouldn't get so jealous. It's not as if I can't be friends with both of you."

"Oh yes it is," muttered Alison. But that wasn't the point. The point was that Sharkey and Black Beauty were crouching under the picnic table on the deck. Ready for the aliens to beam down.

"Where's your sister?" Denise asked, as if Alison hadn't said anything. "I have to explain to her about the music and when to hold up the scorecards and everything."

They found Maureen watching TV in Mom and Dad's bedroom, with her feet on the pillows and her chin propped in her hands. "Not right now," she told Denise without looking at her. "I've got to see what's happening with Felicia and Frisco."

"I guess we just can't have the pageant today, then," said Alison with relief. "Maureen's awfully stubborn about 'General Hospital.'"

"That's ridiculous." Denise stood in front of the TV, glaring at Maureen through her glasses until the older girl rolled off the bed.

"Oh, all right." Maureen gazed at Alison as if she'd just remembered something important. "There's someone I have to keep an eye on anyway."

"Aren't you going to get dressed up to be a judge?"

Denise looked pointedly at Maureen's boxer shorts and old T-shirt and bare feet. Maureen gave Denise a haughty stare, but she went into her room and got a short black jacket and a black hat.

As Denise was showing Maureen the scorecards—cardboard from laundered shirts numbered with a felt-tip marker—the doorbell rang. "That must be Sonia," said Denise eagerly.

It was Sonia, waiting outside the screen door and fluffing her clouds of light brown hair so that they stood out around her sharp face even more. She was wearing a leotard and shorts, like Denise, and carrying a gym bag. Behind her were Karen and her cousin, also in leotards and shorts, glancing sideways at Sonia.

"Hi," said Denise breathlessly, opening the door for Sonia.

"Hi hi hi!" Smiling as if she were being filmed by a camera crew, Sonia walked into the kitchen. She looked like a person on TV, too, her eyes and cheeks and lips bright with makeup.

Alison felt an urge to push Sonia right back out the door. She never would have invited Sonia over, never. But here Sonia was, walking in as if it were an honor to Alison to have her.

Denise led the girls into Alison's bedroom, where Sonia, Karen, and Karen's cousin, Ellie, put their bags down. For a moment no one said anything. Usually Karen would have been the one to crack a silly joke and make everyone feel more at ease, but today she looked shy. So did her cousin. Denise glanced at Sonia, waiting for her to speak.

Sonia gazed slowly around Alison's room. "Curious George," she said, raising her eyebrows at the stuffed animals on the bed. "Candy," she added, with a pained laugh, looking up at a mobile of chocolates. Denise had given Alison that mobile for her birthday.

Looking uncomfortable, Denise opened her mouth and then shut it again. Nobody else spoke as Sonia took a large can of Heavenly Hold hair spray from her gym bag. Gazing in the mirror over the dresser, she fluffed her hair and sprayed it. Then she turned and struck a pose like a jazz dancer. "Are we ready?"

Denise cleared her throat. "Everyone except the MC. Well, come on in the living room and see how I set up for the pageant." Karen and Ellie trailed after them, but Alison stayed to change into her host outfit.

Buttoning Denise's brother's white shirt, Alison wondered why she was letting the pageant go on. Because it looked like no matter what happened, this would be the end of her friendship with Denise. It was sickening, the way Denise looked at Sonia. So admiring, so eager to please. If the pageant went well, Sonia *would* be pleased with Denise and they'd be closer than ever. If it didn't, Denise would blame Alison and her "pretending."

As Alison dragged her feet down the hall to the living room, she heard Denise's eager voice speaking to Sonia. "Don't you wish there was going to be an audience? Maybe we could do this again for Rushfield TV or something."

Sonia smiled as if she thought she would be a big hit on TV. But Karen grinned and poked Ellie. "I don't

wish there was an audience. There might be boys!"
She and her cousin burst into giggles.

Sonia gave Denise a pained look that said, Not very
mature. With a glance at Karen's ordinary sneakers,
she remarked, "I thought everyone was going to buy
aerobic shoes for the ensemble dance number."

Denise looked as shocked as Alison felt. Karen's family didn't have much money; Sonia should know that.

"Anyway," said Denise to cover up, "the main thing
is poise. This is just practice, but Rushfield TV might
really want to put it on."

Karen turned red, staring down at her sneakers. She
looked as if she might burst out with something, but
just then Maureen strolled into the living room wearing her black hat. Gazing at Sonia through dark
glasses, she raised an eyebrow. Then she settled herself
on the sofa with the cardboard scorecards on her stomach and her bare feet on the coffee table.

"I told you I'd get a mature judge," said Denise
proudly to Sonia.

Then Denise ushered Sonia and Karen and Ellie into
the hall, whispering instructions. "We have to wait
until the MC introduces us. Then we do our group
dance number. Go on, Alison."

Alison hadn't been nervous at all, since she knew
there wasn't any audience. But as she stepped onto
the hearth, in front of the palm-tree shower curtain,
she suddenly felt self-conscious. As if there were un-
seen watchers, like a TV audience. The suit she had on
was too hot for this July day, and the "spotlight" from
the gooseneck lamp made it even hotter. Alison's neck
itched under the stiff shirt collar.

Glancing to her left, through the sliding door to the deck, Alison saw that someone besides Maureen was watching her. Sharkey crouched in the shade of the picnic table with his striped tail out behind him and his head on one side. HELP, BIG MAMA, she imagined him calling.

At the sight of her cat, Alison felt a pang. When she had found Sharkey on Tuesday, she thought she could solve all his problems by loving him and giving him a good home. She didn't know then that Sharkey was in much worse trouble than she had ever dreamed of—that the aliens had found him first.

"Start, Alison," whispered Denise.

Alison pulled her thoughts away from Sharkey and raised her script. "Good afternoon, everyone, and welcome to the world premiere of the first annual Miss Preteen Rushfield beauty pageant!" she read into the floor lamp–microphone.

"How can it be a world premiere, if it's just Rushfield?" asked Maureen.

"I didn't write it," said Alison.

"I can't believe this," said Sonia to Denise.

Quickly, before Denise could get upset, Alison read on. "Please welcome our lovely contestants with a big hand!"

Tucking the script under her arm, Alison started to clap. But then she stopped, realizing that the girls weren't dancing into the living room as they were supposed to.

Denise stuck her head around the corner. "Maureen!" she whispered. "The tape, remember?"

"Oh, silly me." Maureen stretched one leg over the

side of the sofa to reach the play button on the stereo with her big toe. Music began to play: Prince, singing "U Got the Look."

"Turn it up!" whispered Denise. But Maureen shook her head, pointing down in the direction of Mrs. Harrity's office.

Sonia pranced in first, smiling into the spotlight and making gestures Alison recognized from rock videos. "Unsavory," Denise's mother would have called that way of dancing. Then came Denise, looking quite different without her glasses.

But it wasn't just no glasses and a lot of makeup, thought Alison. Denise was smiling in a weird way, as if she had twice as many teeth as usual. And she seemed to be trying to dance like Sonia, although it looked more like she was making fun of her. Alison saw Maureen snickering to herself, and she felt embarrassed for her friend.

"Now we each introduce ourselves," called Denise to Sonia and Karen and Ellie over the music. "Keep on dancing." She stepped onto the hearth beside Alison, and smiled even more toothily at a point over the sofa. "I'm Denise Farino, from Cedar Lane!"

Denise danced off the hearth. One at a time Sonia and Karen and Ellie stepped up and introduced themselves to the imaginary audience.

Then the four contestants ran back to Alison's room to change into their swimsuits. Even before they were out of the living room, Maureen started to snort with laughter.

But Alison's mind was far from Maureen sneering at

their beauty pageant. She'd decided what she would do to "mess things up" for Marvin. Alison hurried out to the kitchen, checking to make sure the other girls were all in her bedroom with the door shut, and dialed Marvin's number.

She would demand that Marvin "communicate" with the Aldebarans to take Sharkey's collar off. If Marvin said no, Alison wouldn't let him even step on the deck, where he was expecting to hold his meeting, "bigger than the first moon landing," with the aliens. That would fix him.

"I'm afraid Marvin can't talk to you right now," Mrs. Smith told her. "He gets so wrapped up in his science projects! He asked me not to disturb him."

"But this is very, very, very important," pleaded Alison. "I'm sure he'd—"

"Don't take it personally, dear," said Marvin's mother. "Scientists are like that. I'll tell him you called when he—"

There was a brief pause, and then Marvin came on the phone. "I was just going to call you. You've got to bring the computer upstairs so it'll be ready."

Alison, about to announce her demand, was caught off guard. "Bring the computer! Are you crazy? We were lucky Mom didn't kill us for using the computer again last night."

"I have to use my computer program to communicate with them." Marvin's tone said that Alison should know that without having to be told. "Put the computer in the kitchen—no, the living room . . . Wait a minute! Do you have an outlet on the deck? That would be perfect."

Alison sputtered, but Marvin didn't seem to notice. "So, I'm coming right over," he went on. "If the Aldebarans show up, stall them until I get there."

· 15 ·

A Surprise Audience

Alison felt so off balance that she almost let Marvin hang up. But then she recovered herself. "Just a minute!" she screamed. "What about the collars? If they aren't going to take Sharkey's collar off, you can just forget—"

"Calm down," said Marvin. "I discussed that with them—no problem. They'll take the cats' collars off when I meet them."

Marvin hung up. Alison stood staring blankly at the phone. No problem?

"What're you doing?" Denise was at Alison's elbow, wearing a swimsuit and a broad ribbon of shelf paper with the words "Miss Cedar Lane." "We're starting the swimsuit competition right now."

"Who cares?" Alison started to say, but then she shut her mouth and followed Denise back into the living room. She should relax a little—Marvin was actually finally doing something about getting Sharkey's collar off. Now she just had to wait for him to get here.

Sonia and the other girls were fidgeting outside the living room door. The air was heavy with hair spray, and Alison saw that Sonia had stuck her can of Heavenly Hold on the mantel.

As Alison took her place on the hearth, something puzzling occurred to her. How would the Aldebarans know which human was Marvin? To aliens, humans might all look alike, the way the little gray aliens in the *Weekly Informer* all looked alike.

"Put on the swimsuit competition music," whispered Denise to Maureen from the living room door. Maureen had to sit up this time and put a different tape in the tape deck.

Alison looked down at her script. "Ladies and gentlemen, you're in for a treat. Our winsome contestants, dressed for a dip!"

As the strains of Madonna singing "Crazy for You" filled the room, the four contestants wobbled in on their high heels. That is, Denise and Karen and Ellie wobbled, while Sonia turned gracefully this way and that, posing. Over their bathing suits each of them wore a paper ribbon like Denise's, printed with the name of her street.

Alison, reading from her script, announced each girl as she walked past the hearth. Sonia's description read "the very lovely Miss School Street," while Denise was supposed to be "the lovely Miss Cedar Lane." Karen was "poised and pretty Miss Heron Pond Road," and Ellie was only "attractive Miss Summer Street."

Ellie lost one of her high-heeled sandals as she stepped onto the hearth, and she could hardly stop giggling long enough to speak. Sonia sighed and remarked to the ceiling, "This is so sad. Why did I get into this?"

"Poise!" Denise hissed at Ellie.

But all four of the contestants were chosen as finalists, the script said. When Alison read that announcement, Denise gave a shriek as if she were surprised, and she hugged Sonia.

"Get away from me," said Sonia. "What's the matter with you?"

"We're supposed to do that." Denise looked embarrassed and hurt. "Didn't you see that when we watched the Miss Teen America pageant? We're supposed to cry and hug each other. But if you don't want to," she added quickly, "we can skip that part."

Then the four contestants hurried off to Alison's bedroom to change into their evening gowns. "The next thing's the interview, and then you have to give the scores," Alison told her sister. She slid out of the suit jacket and fanned herself with the script. "What do you have so far?"

Maureen turned off the gooseneck lamp spotlight, gingerly unscrewed the white bulb, and screwed in the pink one. "On a scale of one to ten—Karen is two, Ellie is one and a half, Denise is two-thirds—and Sonia watches too much MTV."

Alison couldn't help giggling. But she said, "Come on, this isn't a real pageant. You have to give everyone high scores."

"Relax." Maureen held up the scorecards Denise had given her. "These only go from ten to eight. But I'm not going to have Sonia win, like she obviously thinks she should. She's conceited enough as it is."

Alison felt uneasy. She'd skipped ahead in the script and found that when Miss Preteen Rushfield was crowned, sure enough, it was the very lovely Miss School Street. "Come on, let her win. Denise went to a lot of trouble to—"

A meow from the deck made Alison turn her head. Sharkey and Black Beauty were creeping from the shade of the picnic table into the bright sunlight. Their tongues were sticking out.

Alison's insides turned to jelly. They were coming. What was she thinking of, letting Marvin invite aliens here? Right *here*. On the deck, a few feet away. "Maureen," Alison gasped. "Please. Help. Look at the cats!"

Maureen gave her sister a now-I'm-sure-you're-crazy stare. But she pushed herself out of the sofa cushions and peered through the slider screen at the two cats on the deck. "Ee-yew! They're both having fits."

"No. Not fits. Impulses, in their brains." Even as she talked, Alison had a hopeless feeling about making Maureen understand what was going on. "The aliens from Aldebaran, they're controlling them. Through the collars. See them sparkling?"

Instead of looking at the cats' collars, Maureen turned to gaze at Alison through her dark glasses. "Allie, don't you get it? Marvin is the one who put the collars on the cats. Marvin's the one who made you think aliens were sending messages to the cats."

"But I *saw* the messages!" exclaimed Alison. "On the computer."

"Oh, right," said Maureen with a pitying smile. "On whose computer? Marvin could make anything come up on that screen. I told you, he wants you to think aliens are coming because he's doing some experiment on how people act when they think aliens are coming."

Alison stood speechless for a moment. The inside of her head felt all jiggled around, as if a picture puzzle had flown apart into hundreds of little pieces and then started to come together again in quite a different way.

"Aliens from *Aldebaran,*" Maureen went on. "Please! He must have gotten that name from a comic book."

"No, it's a real star," said Alison, but she hardly knew what she was saying. Marvin. Yes. He'd done the whole thing himself.

"Oh, there's my hair spray," said Sonia's voice. Alison turned to see Denise's round face next to Sonia's older-looking one at the door to the hall. Denise was wearing a pale pink frilly strapless dress, while Sonia had on a red taffeta dress with thin straps and ruffles.

Maureen strolled back to her place on the sofa, and Sonia gave her hair one last squirt of spray. Just as Denise nodded at Alison to begin the final section of the pageant, Alison glanced back at the cats on the deck.

Poor kitties! Sharkey and Black Beauty were both having full-blown "fits." Their tongues were sticking out, their ears and whiskers twitched crazily. And their collars glowed and flickered much more brightly than before.

How could Marvin do this to these poor cats? When he showed up, Alison was going to tell him just what she thought of him. He probably thought he was brilliant, the way he'd fooled her. Pretending not to know anything about the collars. Pretending to want to read the *Weekly Informer.*

Just a minute. That story in the *Weekly Informer.* Marvin didn't make *that* up.

The puzzle pieces in Alison's mind seemed to fly up in the air and sort themselves out again. Maureen was wrong. She was older and bossier than Alison, and she knew Marvin better—but she didn't understand what was going on now.

"Alison," Denise prompted in an anxious tone.

The aliens are coming. Get everyone out. Alison stumbled off the hearth, toward Denise waiting in the doorway.

"I have to talk to you," gasped Alison. "We can't—"

Denise stuck her frantic face into Alison's "Are you crazy? We're almost at the end of the pageant. You can't talk to me now."

Alison backed away from the unnerving sight of Denise up close with all that makeup on. "But they're coming. You don't—"

"Are we having a beauty pageant, or is this playtime?" demanded Sonia loudly. "If no one else is going to take this seriously, why should I waste my time?"

Putting her arm around Alison, Denise hustled her back in front of the shower curtain. "Listen," she whispered, "I know you don't like it, but please just go ahead and finish, okay?" To Sonia she murmured, with a forced smile, "Sorry."

Helplessly Alison put the suit coat on again and picked up her script. She had the sense of being lifted and carried forward on a giant wave. Whatever would happen, would happen, and Alison couldn't stop it.

"Now we have the opportunity to meet each of our lovely contestants individually, folks," Alison read. "First let's say hello to—Miss School Street, Sonia Best!"

Her bright red taffeta dress rustling with every show-off step, Sonia flounced onto the hearth and into the spotlight from the gooseneck lamp. She smiled with all her teeth toward a point above the sofa, and Alison opened her mouth to ask the first interview question.

"Wait!" Denise stepped into the living room, hitching up the top of her cousin's prom dress. She had pinned the back to make it fit, Alison noticed, but she hadn't quite succeeded. "I'd better—you know, fix this," she said apologetically to Sonia.

Looking pained, Sonia leaned back and shook her hair to fluff it out. "It's not going to make that much difference, and this is taking forever. Why don't you just sort of hold the front of your dress up?" Straightening into dance-class posture, Sonia smiled her toothy smile again.

"Go on," she muttered to Alison through her teeth.

Denise ducked out of the living room, holding her dress in back. Alison hesitated. Should she go on with the show, or wait for Denise to repin her dress?

Sonia cleared her throat in an angry way.

Best to get it over with. With an effort, Alison began to read her script. "Miss School Street, how would you feel if you won—"

Worlworl! yowled the cats. Alison's head whipped around toward the deck.

The air behind Sharkey and Black Beauty was shimmering. It was going to happen right now.

Now. A butterscotch-colored hill, about Alison's height, appeared behind each cat.

Sonia turned and screamed. Karen, peering around the corner from the hall, giggled, then screamed. Ellie screamed and giggled.

Alison wanted to scream, but her breath was gone.

A life-form. The words in the message she and Marvin had seen came to her mind. Those butterscotch-pudding hills were alive. At the base, they were like giant snails without shells. They stared at the girls with eyes placed high on the hill, above their tentacles, which curled and uncurled.

In a moment that seemed to blow up like a balloon until it lasted an hour, Alison's gaze focused on Sharkey and the rubbery pudding-being behind him. A moan choked her throat. The alien was stretching a tentacle down to Sharkey's white neck.

Grab him. Run. Alison's mind gabbled in fast-forward, but her body was stuck in slow-motion time. As Alison began to move toward the sliding door, the alien behind Sharkey lifted its tentacle. It grasped a clear circle—Sharkey's collar.

"Five points off apiece for lack of poise," called Maureen, struggling to sit up straight on the sofa.

But it was Sonia who acted first. "Get out of here, you geeks!" she screamed at the beings on the deck. Yanking open the slider screen, she ignored the white cat streaking into the room. She marched toward the nearest alien with her hand upraised. "You *immature* fifth-grade boys! Go—Ecch!"

Sonia's insults ended in a screech as the alien seized one wrist, then another, with its tentacles. The other alien slithered sideways, surprisingly fast on its snail-like foot. With two tentacles it held up what had been Sharkey's collar and started to force it down over Sonia's head.

· 16 ·

Miss Preteen
Rushfield

In a horrifying flash Alison guessed what must have happened. Of course the aliens would agree to take Sharkey's collar off—because they planned to put it right back on Marvin. That's what they thought they were doing now.

This was an emergency. Alison was the only one who knew what was going on. *Move!* At last her feet moved, lurching her toward the open slider screen.

But in the doorway to the deck she paused, short of breath. She couldn't stop her knees from trembling. She couldn't make herself step within reach of those rubbery tentacles.

Luckily, the aliens were having trouble forcing the collar over Sonia's moussed and scrunched-up and sprayed bunches of hair. Sonia flailed and spit, her hair pushed down over her eyes and into her mouth. "Get away from me!" she snarled, not very clearly.

Throw something! Alison thought. She whirled and

grabbed the nearest objects from the mantel. The crown, the bouquet.

Standing just out of reach, Alison hurled the crown at the alien holding Sonia. It hit the top of its head (if that's what the rounded part above the tentacles was), wobbled, and rested there. She hurled the bouquet. The alien caught the bunch of flowers with an extra tentacle.

Stupid, stupid! Alison seemed to be in a nightmare where she couldn't think straight, couldn't do anything right. Of course the crown and the bouquet weren't heavy enough to hurt anyone, including aliens.

As Alison hesitated, she heard a firm step behind her, and the foamy gurgle of liquid shaken in a can. "Marvin," said Maureen, "this is not funny. You've gone too far." She pushed past Alison and onto the deck.

Alison moaned in horror. She noticed Black Beauty scooting off the deck with her fur all puffed out, while a second collar gleamed in one of the aliens' tentacles. "Keep away from them, Maureen. They're real aliens!" she wanted to yell. But all that came out of her mouth was a choked gargle.

Paying no attention, Maureen pulled the cap off the can of hair spray and pointed the nozzle at the alien pushing the collar down onto Sonia. A cloud of Heavenly Hold rose around the alien's octopus head. Its tentacles shot straight up, quivering. The collar dropped onto the deck.

Alison held her breath, partly with hope and partly because of the hair-spray fumes drifting her way.

Without hesitating, Maureen shifted the spray to the other alien, the one holding Sonia. "That goes for your nerdy friend, too!"

The second alien's tentacles flew up in the air. Sonia stumbled into the living room, coughing.

"Go home!" Alison heard herself shouting, as if the aliens were a pack of dogs. Behind her, Karen and Ellie squealed with delight.

"What's going on?" It was Denise, tottering into the living room on her high heels, still clutching the back of her cousin's prom dress. She grabbed Sonia's arm. "What happened to your hair?"

Sonia jerked her arm away as if Denise had a terrible catching disease. "Did you tell those boys we were having a beauty pageant?"

"They're real aliens," said Alison urgently. How could it be that no one except her realized that? Maureen, still holding the hair-spray can, had actually turned her back on the aliens to watch Sonia and Denise.

Meanwhile, the live butterscotch puddings on the deck were pulling themselves together. They were picking up the two collars from the deck, they were holding them high, the collars were glowing. . . .

The aliens were gone.

Alison made a wordless noise and pointed, but no one paid any attention to her. Denise stared at Sonia as if she'd gone crazy. "What boys? I didn't . . . I just heard you guys screaming."

" 'What boys?' " Sonia echoed her mockingly. "What do you think *that* is?" She jabbed a forefinger at the deck, then dropped her hand. "Well, of course they're gone by now." She didn't seem to notice the two alien-sized slime spots on the gray boards.

"Boys." Karen did a little dance step with delight. "They were *so gross,* Denise! You should have seen them. They had these cool slimy rubber costumes on, and—"

"—and they were doing all these special effects and everything!" Ellie burst in.

Denise peered nearsightedly at the empty deck. "But—but how could boys find out about the pageant?"

"You are so lame, Denise." Sonia's poised 'n' pretty features pulled into a cold scowl. "Couldn't you even keep them from spreading it all over about the pageant?" She waved a hand at Alison and Karen and Ellie, as if they were someone's pesky little sisters.

Now Denise is going to blame me, thought Alison. She knelt beside the sofa where she'd seen Sharkey disappear.

Maureen stepped into the living room, clearing her throat in a take-charge way. "Hey, don't blame Denise," she told Sonia. "I know who those boys were."

Sonia's head jerked around to stare at Maureen. Sonia's eyes widened, then narrowed, as if she thought she understood something. "I *bet* you know them." She turned back to Denise. "A 'really mature' judge, huh?"

Denise flapped her hands in horrified protest, but Sonia went on. "It was a weak idea to have a pageant with you anyway. You can't dance, and your hair's all wrong."

Alison, looking up from beside the sofa, thought that

if Sonia could see her own messy hair, she wouldn't criticize anyone else's. Alison crouched down again and put her hand under the sofa flounce. Sharkey rubbed his whiskers against her fingertips, but he wouldn't come out.

"You and your immature friends in a beauty pageant," Sonia went on. "What a joke."

Denise stared at Sonia, sputtering, then seemed to find her voice. "Well, excuse me for going to all this trouble! *You* aren't as beautiful as you think you are. And if you ask me, there's something unsavory about the way you dance."

Sonia looked ready to give a cutting answer, but Maureen interrupted them. "Listen! The basement door's opening. Mom's coming. I *told* you kids to keep the volume down."

Sure enough, it was Mrs. Harrity stalking down the hall, and she was not pleased. She made everyone leave right away, except for Alison and Maureen. Their mother ordered them to put the shower curtain back in the bathroom, straighten the living room furniture, and clean what Mrs. Harrity assumed were spots of hair spray off the deck.

Maureen helped Alison a little with the furniture, but then she settled herself on the picnic table to watch Alison scrub the deck. Without any discussion, it was understood between the sisters that Maureen had saved the day and shouldn't have to do any work.

Of course Maureen didn't realize how heroic she'd really been, thought Alison as she began to wipe the boards with spray cleaner and paper towels. So far as Maureen knew, she'd only saved Alison from being fooled by one of Marvin's schemes. She'd never believe that she had beaten back an invasion of aliens from Aldebaran.

Giving a short laugh, Maureen pointed across the back lawn. "Look who's returning to the scene of the crime."

It was Marvin, pounding around the corner of the house. "They're not here yet," he said, panting. "Thank goodness. But where's the computer?" He held up his program disk and the wire with the electrodes. "We've got to get the computer upstairs and set up . . ." His voice trailed off as he focused on Sharkey, perched on the deck railing. "Where's his collar?" he demanded, pointing to the cat's bare neck.

"Why, Marvin Smith." Maureen spoke in an interested tone. "What a coincidence. The aliens disappear and you show up, just like that."

"Disappear?" Marvin's Curious George face looked so much like a disappointed monkey's that Alison had to giggle.

"I have to hand it to you," Maureen went on. "Your special effects were incredible. But now why don't you get back in your slimy costume? You look better that way."

Alison knew Denise had been mad at Sonia when she left, but she didn't know how Denise felt about her. She found out the next morning, though, when Denise called to suggest another meeting of what she called "the Secret Readers Club." She added, "I've got dibs on ANCIENT EGYPTIANS KNEW LOVE SECRETS."

"Okay," said Alison, laughing from relief. "Dibs on

ALIEN PLANT MUNCHES—" No. Somehow that story didn't appeal to her anymore. "I'll choose when you get here."

A short while later, Alison heard the crunch of gravel as Denise rode up on her bicycle. "You won't believe this," said Denise, stepping into the kitchen, "but Sonia told me we should put the pageant on again."

"Really?" Alison stared. "I thought she was so mad she'd never speak to you again." She picked up Sharkey, who was rubbing against her ankles.

"Yeah, that's what I thought," said Denise, following Alison to her room. "But she calmed right down after your mother made us leave, and she started walking with me. She said she guessed it was only natural for boys to want to watch her, even if they did have to be so gross about it."

Alison giggled. "She's not too conceited, is she? Maureen's absolutely sure the boys in the alien costumes were Marvin and his friend, doing an experiment on *me*," she went on. "So it didn't have anything to do with Sonia."

"Of course it didn't." Denise sniffed scornfully. "Anyway, then she said I probably didn't let the boys know about the pageant on purpose; it was just one of those exciting things that get around before you know it."

"So what did *you* say?" Alison bent her head over Sharkey, glancing sideways at her friend. She couldn't imagine that Denise would still want to please Sonia. But then, she hadn't imagined that Denise would want to make friends with Sonia in the first place.

Denise pressed her lips together, and her eyes flashed behind her glasses. "I said, 'Good-bye, lovely Miss School Street.'"

Both girls laughed. Then Denise nodded at the red band around Sharkey's white neck. "Sharkey has a new collar."

"Yeah. Dad took me to the pet store last night. And Sharkey's ID tag"—Alison touched the thin metal disk dangling from the collar—"came in the mail this morning, so that worked out perfectly." Everything had worked out perfectly, thought Alison. Here she was, sitting on her bed so comfortably with her best friend Denise and her cat Sharkey.

As if he agreed, Sharkey sighed and settled deeper into Alison's lap. Alison knew exactly what he was thinking:

NO MORE SKY GUYS
NO MORE MOUSE–DUNG COLLAR
BIG MAMA FOREVER

The End

The Aliens Depart

Back in their spacecraft, neither of the Aldebarans made a sign for several minutes. They plunged into the decontamination chamber and let the soothing brown liquid wash off the poisonous spray. But when they were settled again in their resters beside the instrument panel, Commander Xorple turned her cold rubbery-lidded eyes on Instruments Operator Phtui.

You made grave errors regarding the dominant life-form, Operator, she signed with fierce jerks of her forward tentacles.

Phtui shuffled his foot. *Yes, Commander.*

First of all, you assumed that White Cat's life-form was the dominant one just because the cats thought it was. Second, when we made contact with the actual dominant life-form, the humans, you failed to detect their hostility or their possession of a lethal chemical weapon. This will not look good on your permanent record, Operator.

No, Commander. Phtui knew he was in serious trouble, yet he couldn't help being distracted by Commander Xorple's appearance. The Commander didn't seem aware that she was still holding the artifacts one of the humans had hurled at her. She looked very silly with a bunch of soggy imitation plants grasped in a side tentacle and a circle of points stuck on her head.

Phtui might have smiled—if he had had a mouth, and if he could have read the words on the circle perched on Commander Xorple's head: *Miss Preteen Rushfield.*